Goldenrod

Goldenrod

JIM SLATER

Illustrated by
Christopher Chamberlain

JONATHAN CAPE
THIRTY BEDFORD SQUARE LONDON

First published 1978
Text and illustrations © 1978 by Slater Books Ltd

Jonathan Cape Ltd, 30 Bedford Square, London WC1

British Library Cataloguing in Publication Data

Slater, Jim
Goldenrod.
I. Title
823'.9'1J   PZ7.S/
ISBN 0–224–01629–6
Printed in Great Britain by the Anchor Press Ltd
and bound by Wm Brendon & Son Ltd
both of Tiptree, Essex

For Clare, Christopher,
Mark and Jennifer

Contents

Goldenrod

I

Tara's Prophecy

When William Rod was born in the Willingdon Hospital in New Delhi, nobody realised he was blind. It was a day later that the doctor who made routine tests of all new-born babies discovered William was unable to see. Dr Sharma, who attended Mrs Rod during the birth, had the difficult task of telling the truth to William's parents. He was a kind man, always completely honest with his patients, but he had little time for small talk and believed in coming straight to the point.

"It's bad news, I'm afraid," Dr Sharma said, as he entered Mrs Rod's hospital bedroom. "You must prepare yourselves for a shock. Your boy appears to be blind."

Mrs Rod burst into tears. She was still feeling rather weak after William's birth and the shock was too much for her. Mr Rod held her hand; he too felt stunned, but he was naturally anxious to find out if there was any hope for the future.

"Will he ever be able to see?" he asked.

"We'll not be able to tell for another six months. Then you should consult an ophthalmic surgeon to find out the exact nature of the problem. An operation can cure some conditions – your son's might be one of them."

"Who's the best ophthalmic surgeon in India?" Mr
Rod asked.

"Mr Rahim Singh," Dr Sharma replied without hesitation. "He's one of the best in the world."

"That's who we'll see," Mr Rod said, as he turned to
comfort his wife. "Try not to worry, darling, we'll do
everything possible for William."

Three days later Mr Rod drove his wife and new baby
back to their home. As a young man of only thirty-four,
he was lucky to hold an important position advising the
Indian Government on how best to grow more food.
Because of his job, he had to live near New Delhi, the
capital of India, so he rented a modern, air-conditioned
bungalow with a large garden on the outskirts of the city.

They were welcomed home by Pinukhan, their bearer,
who was in charge of the other servants. Standing just
behind him was Tara, William's *ayah*, whose small, frail
body seemed a little lost in her flowing green *sari*. Mrs
Rod passed the baby over to her and she lovingly took
him into her arms. On hearing of his blindness she
had been very upset, but as Tara looked down into
his bright blue eyes, she seemed to see something that
made her deeply lined, brown face light up with happiness.

"Don't worry, *memsahib*," she said. Then she paused
for a moment, closed her eyes, and added mysteriously,
"Before his sixth birthday the *chota sahib* will see better
than all of us."

"What does she mean?" Mrs Rod asked her husband
as Tara carried William away to settle him down in his
new bedroom.

"I don't know, but her elder brother's a famous *fakir*
and all of their family have special powers. Pinukhan

knows about these things and he says she's able to see into the future."

"Do you really believe she can?" Mrs Rod asked hopefully.

"I think it's very likely she's seen something."

"Please have another word with her and find out what she meant," Mrs Rod insisted.

Later, Mr Rod questioned Tara, but she only had a hazy recollection of what had happened.

"I must have been in a trance, *sahib*," she explained.

"Tara, can you remember saying that the chota sahib will see better than all of us?" he asked.

"I don't remember what I said, sahib, but I know that when he sees, it will be differently from other people."

Mr Rod pressed Tara further.

"What do you mean, 'differently'?" he asked.

"Better, sahib. Better," she replied.

Tara's prophecy didn't surprise Mr Rod; it comforted him. He knew that many strange and mystical things happened in India. He had seen a fakir walk on burning coals and had heard stories about them eating fire and being buried alive.

Mr Rod believed in the mystical, but he was also a positive thinker. He never just sat back and waited for things to happen to him; he always did everything in his power to overcome his problems. But for six months there was nothing he could do about William's blindness. Mr Rod knew that while he and his wife waited to consult Mr Rahim Singh the time would pass very slowly.

2

The First Gift

Six months later Mr and Mrs Rod returned to the Willingdon Hospital to consult Mr Rahim Singh. He was called Mister instead of Doctor because he was a surgeon. Only those doctors who pass further difficult examinations and then become surgeons obtain the distinction of being able to call themselves Mister.

Of course the important thing is not what people are called but the kind of person they are and how good they are at their jobs. Mr Rahim Singh was one of those men everyone respected: he knew all about eyes and was without doubt the greatest ophthalmic surgeon in India. He was short, with iron-grey hair, a small moustache, and intelligent brown eyes which twinkled behind his tortoise-shell spectacles. As he came into his hospital consulting-room the nurse almost curtsied, she was so in awe of him; even Dr Sharma hardly dared speak when Mr Rahim Singh was present.

"It's very good of you to see us," Mr Rod said.

"I have examined your son's eyes," Mr Singh replied. "The retinas are not working properly. He can tell the difference between light and dark, but he is almost blind. Fortunately it's an operable condition. I recommend

surgery in about five years' time—it wouldn't be safe before then."

"Thank God," Mrs Rod said joyfully.

Her husband remembered Tara's prophecy and felt very relieved and happy.

"What are the chances of success?" he asked.

"I will perform the operation myself, and I am reasonably confident that all will be well. There is at least a seventy per cent chance that your son will be able to see quite normally afterwards."

Then Mr Singh went on to say something which proved to be very true and of great importance to William's future.

"I know it is difficult for you both now, but while you wait for William to have this operation try not to worry too much. You may find that your son is gifted in other ways – blind children often are."

At the time William's parents didn't pay much attention to Rahim Singh's wise words, but they had cause to remember them later.

The first year of William's life wasn't very different from that of other children. As he was lying in a pram most of the time, being blind wasn't much of a handicap. But when William learned to walk, he had the extra problem of not knowing where things were, and he often bumped into tables and chairs and other unexpected hazards.

"Tara, Tara," he would call, and she was always there. To her the chota sahib was someone very special, and because of his blindness the bond between them became even closer.

By the time he was three, William was able to go from room to room on his own, although Tara had to be hovering within calling distance, ready to help him out of difficulty. He always wanted to explore and it was impossible for Tara to keep her eye on him every minute of the day.

"I only turn my head for a second and he's gone," she complained to William's mother.

But she said it in a proud way; she admired his spirit and was secretly pleased that, in spite of his blindness, he was so energetic and unafraid.

It wasn't until William was four that he could find his

way around the house without any help; by then his mother and father had decided that the only way to deal with the problem was to keep each piece of furniture in exactly the same place. William soon learned where everything was and after that they were careful not to move anything without telling him.

Because he was blind, William's blue eyes had an expressionless look, and when he smiled it made him seem rather sad. Most boys' smiles have a cheeky quality about them, but William's blindness made it difficult for him to get up to any real mischief. He was happiest when people read to him and when Tara and Pinukhan told him some of their wonderful stories about India. It was very difficult for William to imagine what anything looked like, so Tara and Pinukhan took a long time describing the appearance of the animals, people, and surroundings in the tales they told him. After a while William had his own mental pictures – his own ideas of elephants, tigers, dogs, birds, butterflies and trees.

He looked forward most of all to his father's coming home. Mr Rod made up some thrilling adventure stories, and loved to see his son's face light up with pleasure as he told them to him every evening. He had the knack of reaching a very exciting part just as it was time for bed. Then William would find the following day very long, as he waited for the moment when his father would begin the next instalment.

Late one afternoon a few days after William's fourth birthday, Mrs Rod noticed that he was in the hall waiting to welcome his father home.

"Daddy won't be back for an hour yet," she said.

"He's coming now," William replied.

The First Gift

Mrs Rod looked outside. Although there were many palm trees, some dwarf willows and bamboos and a large banyan tree in their garden, she was able to see right to the end of their long drive. There was no sign of her husband's car.

"He won't be home until six o'clock," she said with certainty.

It was a great surprise to her when, two minutes later, Mr Rod arrived. An important meeting had finished earlier than expected and on the spur of the moment he'd decided to come straight home.

"How did you know Daddy was coming?" she asked her son.

"I heard his car," William replied.

"That's impossible," said his mother.

It was only afterwards, when they discussed it together, that his parents realised Mr Rahim Singh had been right: William had a gift. They tried to be casual about it as they didn't want to alarm their son by making him feel there was anything wrong with his hearing. The following day they went into the garden, where they suggested to William that they should play a game.

Mrs Rod sat with her son in the shade of their banyan tree while her husband stood about ten paces away.

"William," Mr Rod said, "I'm going to walk down the garden. I shall keep talking, and you let Mummy know as soon as you can't hear me."

"All right, Daddy," William replied.

Feeling rather foolish, Mr Rod began to recite "Humpty Dumpty", and soon found that he wasn't absolutely sure of the words. He changed to "Jack and Jill". By the time he had finished he was already out of his wife's earshot. Mr Rod decided that nursery rhymes weren't his strong point, so he began to count very slowly up to ten.

When he was about seventy metres away, he called to his wife, "Can he still hear?"

"Daddy's counting. He just said seven," William told his mother before she could say a word.

"Yes," Mrs Rod shouted.

Very slowly Mr Rod continued to widen the distance between them. He kept counting up to ten, and when he had taken another thirty paces he paused for a moment.

"What was the last number?" he shouted to his wife.

"Five," William replied without a moment's hesitation.

"Five," Mrs Rod shouted.

Mr Rod gave the thumbs up sign and resumed his slow backward march. He finally reached William's limit when he was about 150 metres away. Both he and his wife were astonished: even at that incredible distance, if he tried hard William was still able to hear what his father said.

Blind people often develop very good hearing, but William's was extraordinary. It was the first of his three special powers.

3
Mr Singh Operates

It was a pity William couldn't see Tara's big smile as she came into his room to waken him on the morning of his fifth birthday.

"Happy birthday, chota sahib," she said. "Mummy and Daddy have a big surprise for you. *Juldi, juldi,* and get ready before they come."

William jumped out of bed and Tara helped him dress before his parents arrived.

"Happy birthday, darling," his mother said. "Can you guess what we've brought you?"

William didn't have to guess. He had already picked up the sound of an animal moving towards him. He put out his hand and a wet nose pressed against it. They had given him a dog.

With a squeal of delight William threw his arms around him.

"What a wonderful present," he said excitedly. "What kind of dog is it? What's his name? How old is he?"

"Not so fast," his father replied. "One question at a time. He's a golden retriever and his name's Rajah—just like an Indian prince."

"What a super name," William replied, reaching

down to stroke him. His hands moved lovingly over the dog's silky coat.

"Rajah's nearly two years old and he's been trained as a guide dog," Mr Rod said. "The kennels gave us a special whistle, so high-pitched that human ears won't be able to hear it. But Rajah will, and he's trained to come immediately."

"Can I try it now?"

"No, no, we must have breakfast first. Then we'll go into the garden and see how far away he can hear us."

William ate his breakfast very quickly that morning, and was soon in the garden with his father and Rajah. It didn't take them long to discover that the dog could hear his whistle over 300 metres away.

William was thrilled with his new friend, and Rajah immediately sensed that William was his master. During the year that followed they became constant companions. Rajah was always gentle and protective with William, almost as if he knew he was blind.

Mr and Mrs Rod had kept in close touch with Mr Rahim Singh by taking their son twice a year to the hospital for a check-up. When William was nearly six, Mr Singh informed them that he was old enough to have the operation on his eyes and he would have a good chance of being able to see perfectly afterwards.

The day before he was due to go into hospital Tara tried to reassure William.

"Have no fear, chota sahib," she said. "All will be well."

"How do you know, Tara?" he asked.

"When I first held you in my arms, I saw you in the future and you could see."

William wanted to believe in Tara, but he still felt frightened by the thought of the operation. He had over-heard his mother tell a friend that it was her son's only chance of gaining his sight.

Mrs Rod took William to the hospital late one hot summer afternoon. She helped him undress and he climbed into bed. His mother read to him for a while, and then he had a light supper. An hour later, when Mrs Rod left, he was already drifting off to sleep.

The following morning Mr Rahim Singh performed the operation. Afterwards William had to lie still in bed for seven long days with his eyes covered by bandages. Although his parents were frequent visitors, he would have had a very dull time if the nurses hadn't spoilt their young patient. They took it in turns to read to him each day, and sometimes the sister would come and tell him stories.

Everyone did their best to keep William happy, but there was a growing feeling of tension in the hospital as the day approached when his bandages were to be removed. Although the nurses didn't talk about it much, they were all anxious to know the result of William's operation.

Mr and Mrs Rod were with Mr Rahim Singh when he carefully unwrapped the bandages. William only had a vague idea of his parents' appearance; he had been told his father was over six feet tall with light-brown hair and blue eyes, and that his mother was quite small and very pretty. He knew she had long hair because he had felt it with his hands often enough. She had told him it was auburn, but when you have been blind from birth words like blue, brown and auburn don't mean very much. It's very difficult to describe colours to someone who has never seen them. William was naturally thrilled at the prospect of gaining his sight and one of the most exciting things about it was that today might be the first time he would see his own mother and father.

Mr Singh finished his task and stepped back. William blinked before slowly opening his eyes. He said nothing for a few seconds and then shouted excitedly:

"I can see! Mummy, Daddy, I can see!"

Mr and Mrs Rod were so thrilled they could hardly speak; then suddenly everyone was talking at once, and the good news began to spread through the hospital.

"Do we look like you expected?" his mother asked.

"You look just like I thought you would, Mummy, but Daddy is taller and much bigger."

They all laughed.

"You'll be able to go home in a few days' time," Mr Singh said.

"Oh good, I can't wait to see Rajah and Tara."

"There's so much to show you," his father said. "We won't know where to begin. I'll have that week's holiday I've been promising myself, so I can enjoy it all with you."

"You told me all about colours," William exclaimed. "But I'd no idea they were so bright and there were so many of them."

"There's so much you'll enjoy now," Mrs Rod said happily. "So many things you'll be able to do. We must go shopping together and buy lots of books. Soon you'll be able to read them yourself."

"I think you should leave him now," Mr Singh said with a smile. "He's had enough excitement for one day. He must rest."

"Oh no, I feel fine," William said happily. But his

parents agreed with the surgeon and went home to give
the good news to Tara. Not that she needed to be told.
She was waiting for them with a happy smile on her face;
it was obvious that somehow she already knew.

A few days later William returned home, very im-
patient to see Rajah and Tara for the first time. Although
he had never seen a dog before, he had a picture of
Rajah in his mind. He knew he had four legs, a silky
coat and a long bushy tail, but he couldn't imagine his
face.

Rajah was waiting for William in the garden. Quickly
realising it was a special occasion, the dog bounded
towards him.

"Isn't he beautiful?" William exclaimed, throwing his
arms around the dog's neck. "I love his face– he looks
so kind and friendly."

William's parents didn't need to speak; they knew
each other's thoughts. The sight of their son playing with
his dog brought tears of happiness to Mrs Rod's eyes.
Another person who was on the verge of crying was
Tara; she had come down from the bungalow and was
patiently waiting until William noticed her. He must
have sensed her presence, because he looked up suddenly.

"You're Tara!" he shouted, as he rushed towards her.

"Welcome home, chota sahib," she said, hugging him
to her.

"I'm so happy, Tara," William said. "You always
told me I'd see."

"Yes, chota sahib. I knew you would. You're almost
ready now," she replied mysteriously.

The small boy could hardly wait to get up the following morning. He found the next few days full of joy. He

had never imagined how beautiful the world was: the bright green parakeets; the sapphire blue trumpet-shaped flowers of the morning-glory vine; the brilliant red flowers of the flame tree; the delicate and gloriously coloured wings of butterflies; their banyan tree's strange way of growing ever wider as some of its branches took root in the soil and became new trunks; the greenness of the grass and the vivid blue of the sky; the way people's faces showed kindness—even just to see someone smile—all of these things were new and wonderful to William.

When a young boy sees for the first time he naturally thinks other people see everything in exactly the same way. That is why many people never know they are colour-blind or only find out after many years. William could see as well as everyone else, but he didn't realise he had an extra gift. When William narrowed his eyes and really concentrated he could see right through solid objects. He didn't mention this to anyone as it never occurred to him that seeing through a wall or a door was in any way unusual. He assumed everyone could do it. Only Tara and her brother, the fakir, were aware that he had been given another special power to help him in the many adventures he would have in the years ahead.

4
The Flower Game

A few months after William's operation his father came home with some wonderful news.

"Guess what?" he said to his wife. "The American Embassy school has a vacancy and they'll take William as a pupil next term."

"I thought they only took children of Embassy officials and American businessmen?" Mrs Rod replied.

"No—they give first priority to Americans, but they accept some other children as well. It should prepare him well for school in England, if ever we go back there."

Both William and his mother were thrilled with the news. Mrs Rod had helped William all she could to learn his letters and to start reading, so she was hopeful he would soon catch up with the other children.

At the beginning of the new term his mother took him to school and introduced him to his form mistress, who was American. William was very relieved to see she was fat and jolly, as he had been worried she might be rather grim.

"Good morning, William. I'm Miss Bunting," she said with a friendly smile. "That will be your desk in the corner. Would you like to go and sit down now? I'll

introduce you all to each other when everyone's here."

William sat in the far corner, where he was soon joined by an American boy who had red hair, freckles and a very cheeky smile.

"What's your name?" the boy asked.

"William Rod—what's yours?"

"John Evans Junior—but all my friends call me Fleabag."

William laughed.

"How did you get a name like that?" he asked.

"From a television serial. You can call me Fleabag if you like. Do you have a nickname?"

"No," William replied, totally unaware that by the end of the day he would have acquired the nickname that was to stay with him for the rest of his schooldays.

After everyone had arrived William quickly counted the girls and boys in his class. The boys were out-numbered by twelve to eight. In front of him sat two girls, Susie and Joanna. He particularly liked Susie, who was a pretty American girl with short dark curly hair; she seemed full of fun and kept turning round to talk to William and Fleabag.

Miss Bunting called the class to order and asked them to stand up in turn and say their names. Afterwards they started their first lesson. William was just beginning to think that his standard of reading wasn't too far behind the other children, when he noticed something very strange in his text-book. He plucked up courage and put up his hand.

"Yes, William?" the teacher said.

"Miss Bunting, I think my book's wrong," William replied. "They've spelt the word colour without the 'u'."

Miss Bunting smiled. "It's an American text-book, William," she said. "In America colour is spelt like that. American spelling is more direct, more as words sound. Programme, for example, is spelt p-r-o-g-r-a-m, not -m-m-e, and theatre is spelt t-h-e-a-t-e-r."

"Miss Bunting, don't English people have different names for some things too?" Susie asked.

"Yes, I can think of a few," she replied. "They call an apartment a flat; a purse a handbag; the sidewalk the pavement; an elevator a lift—and I seem to remember they call the trunk of a car the boot."

William began to think that in addition to his other lessons he might have a difficult time learning to speak American. But then Miss Bunting caught sight of his expression.

"Don't worry, William," she said. "There aren't very many words that are different. If you find any more, just let me know and I'll explain them to you."

School only lasted until one o'clock each day. Then, because of the heat, the children went home for their siestas. Ever since William could remember, his parents had always insisted that between two and four he had a sleep. Just before the bell rang Miss Bunting suggested playing a game.

"Starting with you, Mary, and going along the front row and then the next one, I want each of you in turn to name a flower," she said. "As soon as you can't think of one you drop out and the turn passes on. The last person left in will be the winner."

"Miss Bunting, are they only Indian flowers or can we have American ones too?" Fleabag asked.

"You can name flowers from any country you like, provided I've heard of them. Off you go then, Mary."

It was soon down to Susie and a girl named Rebecca. Susie knew a large number of Indian flowers and in the end she won.

"Well done, Susie, and you too, Rebecca," Miss Bunting said. "I'm rather surprised that you of all people, William, didn't remember one flower—it grows in England as well as America."

"I've never been to England," William replied.

"Oh, I hadn't realised that. Let's see if anyone else knows. It's a tall plant with flowers of the same golden colour as William's hair and part of its name is the same as his surname. Well? Does anyone know?"

Susie put up her hand.

"Yes, Susie?"

"Is it Goldenrod?" she asked.

"That's right—Goldenrod," Miss Bunting said as everyone started laughing.

Fleabag turned to William.

"Now you've got a nickname," he said. "Goldenrod—it's better than Fleabag!"

From that day onwards William was known to his friends as Goldenrod. The name suited him, perhaps because it sounded magical and adventurous. William had already acquired two exceptional powers of a mystical nature; his third and final power was to be the most important one of all.

5
Training Rajah

Goldenrod found that the weekdays went by very quickly. He loved school and was very popular with everyone in his class; except for Gregory Hurst, who was always trying to tell the other children what to do.

Fleabag was quite small and Gregory often picked on him. Goldenrod was taller than Gregory so he was able to come to Fleabag's rescue. Then one day Goldenrod had an idea for dealing with Gregory.

"Fleabag, I've been thinking," he said. "Why don't you ask your father for some special words to say to Gregory next time he tries to order you about?"

"What kinds of words?" Fleabag asked.

"Words he won't understand. He's not really a bully—he's just bossy. He won't like you using lots of words he doesn't know. Maybe he'll leave you alone then."

The next day Gregory tried to stop Fleabag joining in a game some of the boys were playing during break. Then Fleabag said the special words in a loud voice and very superior tone:

"It's not your fault, Gregory, that your character has been spoiled because it's been subjected to genetic and hereditary influences entirely beyond your personal control."

Goldenrod was proud of Fleabag; he said the words as

33

if he had just thought of them. In fact it had taken him nearly an hour to learn their proper pronunciation.

Gregory looked just like a bull that has charged at a matador, and found he is no longer behind his red cape. "Have you swallowed a dictionary?" he asked. "What's all that mean?"

Fleabag, the matador, drew his sword for the kill.

"You mean you don't know?" he said pityingly. "That's part of your problem!"

That was quite enough for Gregory. He never picked on Fleabag again. Only Goldenrod dared to ask what the special words really meant.

"My father says they mean it's Gregory's parents' fault he's so dumb," Fleabag explained. "Don't tell anyone else."

Fleabag and Goldenrod soon became firm friends and quite often went to each other's homes. Although Goldenrod liked school it was the weekends he looked forward to most. On Saturdays after siesta time his father's Indian friend, Jaglish Swami, frequently came to their bungalow, bringing with him his young son, Subash. The two men then went to their club to have their regular games of tennis and snooker, leaving Goldenrod and Subash playing together. Subash was the same age as Goldenrod and always getting into trouble.

While he had been blind Goldenrod hadn't been able to enjoy Subash's company to the full. Subash had often come to spend afternoons with him, but there had been very few games they could play together. Now they enjoyed flying their kites, exchanging stamps, playing marbles, and whipping those large spinning tops that are so popular with children in India. Sometimes Mrs Rod took them to the river Yamuna, where they could fish, and on other occasions they went to the Zoological Park or to an open-air swimming pool.

Goldenrod was very fond of Subash because he was always having new ideas for games and knew plenty of tricks to play on people. Goldenrod had become mischievous; now that he could see, he felt he had some catching up to do, and Subash was just the right boy to help him.

One hot summer's afternoon Fleabag joined them both in the garden.

"Let's give Rajah a bath," Subash suggested.

"That's a good idea," Fleabag said.

Goldenrod agreed and went to find the hose. He soon came back with it holding the nozzle in his hand. Rajah loved his daily bath. As soon as he saw the hose, he rushed towards his master and chased him around the lawn, leaping up at the jet of water. Within a few minutes he was wet and bedraggled, but still game for more.

"You look as if you need a bath, Fleabag," Goldenrod said, flicking the water in his direction.

Subash roared with laughter, until he found that he was the next target. Goldenrod chased them around the garden, but then Subash surprised him by rushing forward quickly and grabbing the hose.

"Now it's your turn," Subash yelled gleefully.

A few minutes later the boys were all drenched. They agreed a truce. As they sat drying off in the sun, a soft voice disturbed them.

"Your mother asked me to bring you some lemonade and biscuits, chota sahib," Pinukhan said.

"Thanks, Pinukhan, that's a super idea," Goldenrod replied.

Before returning to the house, Pinukhan crouched

down and began to talk to Rajah in Hindi. Rajah looked up at him as if he understood every word.

There are only two types of people in this world – those who like dogs and those who don't. And dogs too have their likes and dislikes. Pinukhan was one of those people all dogs like. He was tall and dark with friendly brown eyes, and Rajah was always eager to please him, seeming to sense exactly what he wanted him to do.

"Pinukhan, could you make Rajah go to the house and come back again?" Fleabag asked.

"Yes, he could be taught to do that and many other things," Pinukhan replied.

"He already sits and lies down when I tell him to and he always comes to my whistle," Goldenrod said proudly.

"Any dog can be trained to do those things," Pinukhan replied. Then he looked down at Rajah almost as if he was a person. "This dog is very special – he could be trained to take messages and defend you in times of danger."

"That sounds terrific – can we start this afternoon?" Goldenrod asked.

"Yes, chota sahib," Pinukhan smiled. "I can stay with you for half an hour. We'll cut up an old blanket and we'll need your toy gun – the black plastic one you used to play with."

"I know where it is. I'll go and get it," Goldenrod replied.

"I'll try and find a blanket," Pinukhan said, "and then we'll see what Rajah can do."

When they returned, Pinukhan carefully wrapped the piece of material round his arm.

"I'm going to train Rajah to grip my arm in his teeth," he told the boys. "Although we're friends he might get excited and bite too hard, so I always use a piece of blanket when I train dogs to do this."

"Have you trained many, Pinukhan?" Fleabag asked.

"Yes, I helped train dogs for the police."

"Wow!" was Fleabag's only comment.

"First of all, chota sahib, I'll train Rajah to answer my words of command. The Hindi for 'Attack' is 'Halma' and the Hindi for 'Down' is 'Neachu'. When he understands, I'll train him to do it for you."

Pinukhan held the gun in his hand, patted his arm and moved it backwards and forwards trying to tempt Rajah to leap for it. "Halma!" he kept saying. "Halma!"

It took twenty minutes before Rajah finally leapt and caught Pinukhan's arm in his teeth. Even then he wasn't quite sure what was required of him, but, when Pinukhan said "Neachu!" and gave him one of the biscuits, Rajah realised he was on the right track.

"Halma!" Pinukhan said again. Rajah leapt without a moment's hesitation. Pinukhan gave him another biscuit and repeated the exercise. Finally he said to Goldenrod, "Now he's ready, chota sahib. You lie here under the tree as if you're asleep and I'll creep up on you. When I'm near you, shout 'Halma!' to Rajah and we'll see if he does it for you."

Goldenrod lay down under the tree and pretended to be asleep. Fleabag and Subash stood quietly. They too were very interested to see if Rajah would respond to Goldenrod's command.

Pinukhan crept up on Goldenrod who waited until the last possible moment before saying "Halma!" Rajah didn't hesitate, he leapt at Pinukhan like a bullet from a gun. Pinukhan was bowled over; his orange turban almost came off and Rajah lay on top of him, uncon-

cerned about spoiling his smart white tunic. The arm in the blanket was still firmly gripped between Rajah's teeth.

"Neachu!" Goldenrod commanded.

Rajah dropped Pinukhan's arm and came, tail wagging, to his master. Quickly Goldenrod gave him a biscuit.

"Well done, Rajah," he said, patting his head. "Good boy."

"He's a very quick learner," Pinukhan said breathlessly as he brushed himself down.

They practised a few more times until Rajah was fully familiar with his new trick.

"Pinukhan, are there any other things you can teach him?" Subash asked.

"Yes, another afternoon I'll teach him to do this with a knife as well as a gun, but I must go back to my work now," Pinukhan replied.

After that the boys enjoyed several more training sessions with Pinukhan, and Rajah very quickly learned to carry messages from one of them to another and to go home on command. Above all, though, Rajah liked the gun and knife game: it was fun, it was quick and immediately afterwards he was given a biscuit.

None of the boys realised then that two years later Rajah's extra training would help save the lives of more than one hundred people.

6

The Indian Thread Trick

Goldenrod was lucky because his birthday was in April,
the first month of the hot weather, which lasts for six
months in India. Then the monsoon comes and it pours
with rain every day. In July the Rods' garden turned to
mud and the deep ditch in the road outside was usually
filled with water.

The Indian Thread Trick

As William had been blind for his first five birthdays and at the time of his sixth he hadn't many friends, his parents decided to give him a special party on the day he was seven. He invited Subash and another Indian boy named Jat, and all his class from school—even Gregory Hurst. His parents hired some swings, a roundabout and a slide, and the trees in their garden were festooned with fairy lights and Chinese lanterns. The party began at four o'clock, and after a few games all the children had a splendid tea outside on the lawn, with banana sandwiches, blancmanges, jellies and ice-cream and a large birthday cake covered with grey icing and shaped like an elephant.

The most exciting surprise was that Mr Rod had arranged for a demonstration by a snake-charmer, followed by a man with two dancing bears. The snake-charmer had three poisonous snakes, and as he played

his flute they gradually rose up out of their small basket and swayed in time with the music. As it reached a higher pitch, he raised his flute in the air and the snakes followed it upwards hypnotised by the music. The snake-charmer had to keep playing because the moment he stopped the snakes might bite him. But all was well and as he lowered the pitch again, slowly bringing down his flute, the snakes sank obediently back into their basket.

Then it was the turn of the dancing bears. The man played a thalibaja, a kind of small drum, and the two large dark-brown bears danced to its beat. The bears wore golden collars, which had long thin ropes in case they tried to stray. Later the bears entertained everyone by turning somersaults, wrestling and playing with each other until the children's parents arrived to take them home.

Only Subash stayed behind. He was a special friend, and he had some important information for Goldenrod. The two boys quietly slipped away to talk together.

"I did the trick on my parents last week," Subash explained. "It took my father half an hour to find out what it was."

"I've got a drawing pin and some thread," Goldenrod replied. "Will I need anything else?"

"Yes, you'll want a lead weight. I've brought one with me." Then Subash tied the lead weight about thirty centimetres from the end of the thread. "Shall we fix it up now?" he asked.

"Okay," Goldenrod replied. "They won't be going into the sitting-room for a while."

The boys crept around the outside of the bungalow and carefully pushed the drawing pin into the woodwork in the side of the window frame.

"Now, if you pull it taut from your bedroom, the black thread will be invisible in the dark. Then let it go slack and the weight will fall against the window and give it a tap. It drives them mad after a while," Subash explained gleefully.

"Thanks, Subash," Goldenrod said. "I wish you could stay while I try it. I'll let you know what happens in the morning."

The two boys said goodbye. Goldenrod thanked his parents for the party and went to his room. After they had been to kiss him goodnight, he waited for about a quarter of an hour before getting up again. Then he found the end of the black thread, pulled it taut and let it go slack. He repeated the process several times, held the thread taut and awaited developments. Goldenrod concentrated hard; with his very acute hearing he was able to listen to his parents' reactions.

"What's that noise, darling?" Mrs Rod asked.

"The shutter may be loose. I'll have a look," Mr Rod replied, putting down his book and going to the window.

Mr Rod inspected the shutter, which was firmly fastened down. Then he peered out into the gloom but couldn't see anything. He returned to his seat and picked up his book.

Tap, tap, tap.

"There it is again, darling," Mrs Rod said.

Mr Rod sighed. "I've already checked the shutters," he said.

Tap, tap, tap.

Mr Rod marked the place in his book, put it down and went back to the window.

"It may be an animal of some kind," he said. "I can't see anything though."

He waited for a few minutes. Nothing happened, so he returned to his book. He had just picked up the thread of his story when the insistent tapping started again.

Goldenrod was having a fine time. Subash had told him that, to have the maximum effect, it was important to wait a while between taps.

"I'll get to the bottom of this," Mr Rod said, dropping his book in exasperation. "I'm going outside—if you don't hear from me in an hour, send a search party," he added with a smile.

Tap, tap, tap.

"There it is again," Mrs Rod said. In her husband's opinion she wasn't being particularly helpful; he knew that irritating noise well enough.

Mr Rod was soon outside the window waiting in the shadows.

Tap, tap, tap.

This time Mr Rod saw the black thread. Quickly he grabbed it and followed it round to his son's room. Goldenrod felt the pull, dropped the thread and scampered into bed.

A moment later his door opened.

"I've just come to wish you goodnight again," his father said.

Goldenrod pretended to be asleep.

"In case you're awake, William, I want you to know I admire initiative," his father said from the doorway. "But taken too far it makes people angry, and taken further, it leads to enemy action."

No answer from Goldenrod.

"Goodnight, William."

Still no answer.

The day had been wonderfully exciting for Goldenrod,

but even so he soon dropped off into a dreamless sleep. He would have found this far more difficult, if he had known then that Rajah had been in contact with a virus, and would soon become very ill.

7
Rajah's Illness

One Saturday morning two weeks after his birthday party, Goldenrod noticed that Rajah was much less lively than usual. He had seemed a little off colour for some time. Normally Rajah would follow him around eagerly in the hope that they might go for a walk or play a game together, but that morning he was listless and seemed to prefer just sitting in the shade of the banyan tree.

" 'Chalna', Rajah. Chalna!' " Goldenrod called the Hindi word for "Walk", hoping to excite his dog's interest.

Instead of bounding forward and barking joyously, Rajah slowly lifted his body from the ground like a tired old man getting up from his favourite chair.

"What's wrong, boy?" Goldenrod asked, as he stroked his dog's head. Usually that was enough to persuade Rajah to roll over on his back in the hope that Goldenrod would make a real fuss of him. Today he just sat down and looked up at his master with a mournful expression. Golden retrievers have sad faces at the best of times, so when they try to look miserable they have a big advantage over most other dogs. Rajah succeeded in looking as if the world was coming to an end.

Goldenrod called out to his father, whom he could see through the bungalow window.

"Dad, I don't think Rajah's very well. Will you come and have a look at him?"

"I thought he was a bit tired last night," Mr Rod replied as he joined his son in the garden. Then he inspected Rajah carefully.

"I'm no expert on dogs but there's certainly something wrong with him. I might be imagining it but he seems a little thinner than usual. We'll ask the vet to have a look at him."

Rajah had been so fit that he had only seen the vet for routine vaccinations and once when he cut himself badly and had to have three stitches. Then they had consulted Mr Sastri, who lived about four kilometres from their home. Within a few minutes they had Rajah in Mr Rod's car and were on their way to see Mr Sastri again. Goldenrod was very close to his dog and could sense, from his unusually quiet presence in the back of the car, that he was seriously ill.

Mr Sastri was a briskly efficient person. He had a very modern and well equipped surgery. His quietly confident manner began to make Mr Rod and his son feel less uneasy. Then he gave them the bad news.

"I am afraid I don't know exactly what's wrong," he said. "I think he has a viral infection of some kind. I'll give you some antibiotics for him to take regularly to stop a secondary infection developing. He should have a very light diet with plenty to drink. Keep him warm – he may develop a fever later. If he gets over that he'll be all right."

"It all sounds rather vague," Mr Rod replied. "Isn't there anything more you can do?"

"By the time I could identify the virus, the illness will have peaked anyway. I'm sorry I can't be more helpful. I'll try and call in on him tomorrow."

"You take Rajah to the car, William," Mr Rod said. "I want another word with Mr Sastri."

When his son had left the room, Mr Rod asked the vital question.

"You said earlier *if* he gets over the fever he'll be all right – does that mean there's a risk he might not recover?"

"I'm afraid so. It could go either way – viruses can be very tricky. Don't hesitate to call me at any time if he takes a turn for the worse."

That night, Rajah developed a fever and lay shivering under the blanket in his basket. Goldenrod sat close by, occasionally speaking quietly to reassure him, and it was long past his normal time when Mrs Rod insisted that her son went to bed.

"I won't be able to sleep anyway," he replied.

"There's nothing you can do here, William. Your father's asked Mr Sastri to come. You go to bed right away."

Goldenrod gave Rajah a final stroke. He somehow knew that Mr Sastri would be unable to help his dog. Reluctantly he left to prepare for bed. When Tara came to say goodnight, she could see the unhappiness in his face.

"How's Rajah, chota sahib?" she asked.

"He's worse, Tara – much worse."

"Don't worry. I'll go and see my brother tonight. He'll know what to do."

"How can he know what's wrong without even seeing Rajah?" Goldenrod asked.

48

"The vet doesn't know what's wrong and he's seen him, hasn't he?" Tara said. "My brother will see him in his mind. He has great powers and he will know just what to do, You go to sleep and leave it to old Tara."

Goldenrod suddenly realised he was dead tired. He felt very relieved the fakir would soon be helping Rajah. Tara always spoke with such confidence about her brother.

Although his father hadn't told him, he knew instinctively that Rajah's condition was critical. The thought of anything happening to his dog was more than Goldenrod could bear. When he was blind Rajah had been his friend, companion and guide. Now that he could see, there were so many things they could do together and Rajah had become the greatest joy in his life. Wondering anxiously what the next day would bring, he drifted off to sleep.

The following morning Goldenrod went in his pyjamas to the small room adjoining the kitchen to see if Rajah was any better. To his disappointment he looked worse–he had stopped shaking, but was only breathing very shallowly.

"Mr Sastri came last night, William," Mr Rod said from the open doorway behind him. "He's still not sure exactly what's wrong with Rajah, but unfortunately he thinks it's very serious. He's going to arrange for him to be taken to an animal hospital today."

At that moment there was a sound of a key in the lock of the kitchen door. Tara was returning from the visit to her brother.

"Tara, Rajah's worse. They're going to take him to a hospital now," William cried.

"Please don't allow that, sahib," Tara said to Mr Rod.

49

"I've been to see my brother and he's given me some special herbs for Rajah. I'm going to boil them now—he will get better, chota sahib," she added, turning to comfort Goldenrod.

"Dad, I want Tara to look after Rajah, not Mr Sastri," Goldenrod said quietly to his father.

Mr Rod hesitated for a moment before he replied. "He's your dog, William. If that's the way you want it, I'll tell Mr Sastri we'll keep Rajah at home."

Tara put some large leaves that looked like spinach and a variety of other herbs into their biggest saucepan, which she filled with water. As the strange mixture simmered on the stove, a smell rather like asparagus soup began to permeate the bungalow.

"Whatever's that smell?" Mrs Rod asked as she came into the kitchen.

"It's a special mixture for Rajah, memsahib," Tara replied. "It will make him well."

"Tara's been to see her brother," Goldenrod added in explanation.

Mrs Rod decided breakfast could wait, and she had better leave them to it. Rajah came first that morning.

When Tara thought the fakir's medicine was ready, she poured the entire contents of the saucepan into a large jug. Goldenrod was surprised to see that it was only half full of a thick and treacly green liquid. Tara waited for it to cool, and then gave Rajah a teaspoonful.

"He must have it every hour without fail for the next twelve hours," she said.

"He looks terribly ill. Will he be all right?" Goldenrod asked.

Seeing his distress, Tara told him something she might not otherwise have mentioned.

"My brother knows you'll need Rajah in the years ahead," she said. "As he can see him with you in the future, that must mean he's going to get well."

Tara's simple logic and belief in her brother's powers completely reassured Goldenrod. For the first time in twenty-four hours he felt confident that Rajah would recover. Not that there was any visible sign yet – Rajah still looked as sick as ever. His eyes were closed, he was hardly breathing and his tongue was hanging limply from his mouth.

Another hour went by and Tara gave Rajah a further teaspoonful of the medicine. Still no sign of recovery. Another hour passed, and then another. Goldenrod's earlier confidence began to wane. He sat by Rajah's basket and lovingly stroked his dog's head, praying that all would be well.

"William, it's time for lunch," his mother called.

He wasn't hungry, but Tara insisted.

"I'll look after Rajah, chota sahib. It won't do him any good if you don't eat – you go and have your lunch."

When he returned, Tara was just giving Rajah another teaspoonful of medicine. His eyes were open and as he saw his master enter the room he gave a slight whimper. Goldenrod rushed to his side. There was no doubt Rajah had improved.

"He opened his eyes a few minutes ago, chota sahib," Tara said. "I think this is the turning point."

Goldenrod couldn't speak; he felt as if a big weight had been lifted from his back.

'What a pity I wasn't with Rajah when he opened his eyes,' he thought. 'I'd have loved to have been there. Then he'd have known how I feel about him.'

Goldenrod gently stroked Rajah, who lifted his head

slightly. The effort was too much; Rajah closed his eyes and settled into a deep sleep.

"Don't worry, chota sahib," Tara said. "He knows, he knows."

Rajah continued to get better. By the end of the day it was obvious to everyone that he was going to recover. He still looked tired and thinner than usual, but the crisis was over and he was improving rapidly.

Mr Sastri came in to see him again.

"I told you these viruses are tricky," he said to Mr Rod. "You never know where you are with them. They can go either way."

Mr Rod thanked him for his help and smiled at his son. Both of them knew which way it would have gone, if it had been left to Mr Sastri.

That night, when he was about to go to bed, Goldenrod went to thank Tara.

"I'll never forget all you did, Tara," he said. "I'd like to meet your brother to thank him too."

"My brother says you'll be meeting him within a few weeks, chota sahib. He has something to teach you."

She wouldn't say more. So Goldenrod had to go to sleep wondering what she meant.

8

Glowing Green Eyes

Within three weeks Rajah had fully recovered, but then Tara fell ill. Although she was nearly seventy and had never been very strong, everyone was shocked by her sudden disappearance from everyday life at the Rod bungalow. Tara's illness persisted, and it soon became obvious she would have to retire. Mr Rod was happy to pay her a small pension each week, so she decided to go and live with her brother, the fakir.

Goldenrod missed his ayah; life wasn't the same without her. One afternoon a few weeks after her retirement, his mother took him to have tea with Tara. As they waited outside her brother's small house, Goldenrod felt very curious about the fakir, so he narrowed his eyes and used his special vision to look through the thick wooden door. He saw a small wizened man coming down the stairs. He had a thin grey pointed beard, a deeply lined face and was wearing a flowing white robe. After he opened the door, Mrs Rod left them together, promising to call back in two hours' time.

"You must be William," the small man said, as he invited him in. "I have been looking forward to meeting you."

"I'd like to thank you for saving Rajah. He's well again now," Goldenrod said.

"Yes, I know. He is a fine dog," the fakir replied. "I have known for many years that you and I must meet one day. There is something I have to teach you."

"Can I see Tara first?"

"Of course you can," the fakir replied, leading him to an upstairs room where Tara was sitting in bed propped up by several pillows. She looked very frail and ill, but her face lit up at the sight of the boy.

"Ah, chota sahib," she said. "It makes me feel better just to see you."

Goldenrod rushed to her side and gave her a bear-like hug.

"I've brought you some honey, Tara. My mother says it will be good for you."

"Thank you, chota sahib," she said, smiling weakly. "And how is Rajah?"

"He's fine now. Thanks to you and your brother," he replied.

Goldenrod sat for half an hour chatting to Tara, but then he could see she was becoming tired.

"I'd better go and see your brother," he said. "He wants to teach me something. Do you know what it is?"

"Yes, I know all about it," Tara replied. "He's been waiting to meet you for seven years."

Goldenrod quietly left Tara's room and went downstairs. The fakir was waiting for him, sitting cross-legged and motionless on the living-room floor.

"Sit down here, William. I have many things to explain to you."

Goldenrod sat down, crossed his legs and looked into the old man's strange glowing green eyes.

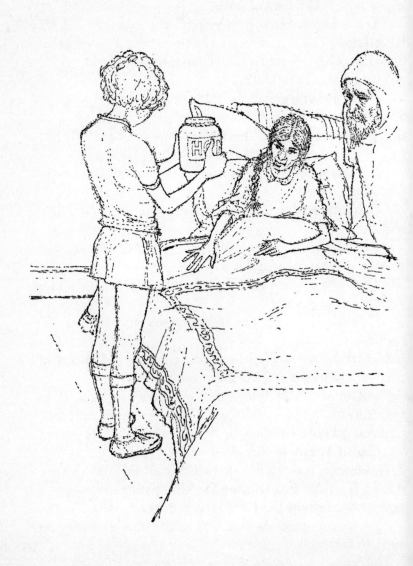

"You are a very lucky boy," the fakir said. "You have been given two special powers."

Goldenrod was aware of one—his exceptional hearing —but he couldn't understand what the fakir meant by saying he had two.

"You have not yet realised that being able to see through things is even more of a special power than your hearing. It is a very important gift and you must never let anyone else know about it."

"You mean other people can't see through walls even if they try really hard?"

"No, even I am unable to do that," the fakir said, smiling at him.

"Why have I got these special powers?"

"That is very easy to answer: you are going to have some great adventures and you will need them to escape from danger. There is one more I am going to teach you —it will be your third and last special power."

The fakir had a very soft voice and to Goldenrod's surprise he spoke excellent English, which, if anything, was rather too perfect and precise. Goldenrod was breathless with excitement; he listened intently, not wanting to miss a word.

"I will teach you to possess in a single minute all the strength you would usually have in one hour. It will make you sixty times stronger than usual, but only for that one minute. Afterwards, you will always feel very weak for about an hour. That is when you will have to be particularly careful."

The fakir explained that it would take several months to teach Goldenrod to concentrate in a very special way, so he would be able to acquire great strength at will.

"Before we begin," he said, "I am going to put you

into a deep hypnotic trance. Then I will give you extra strength for one minute so that you will know exactly how it feels. After that I will teach you to do it without my help."

Goldenrod had never been hypnotised before, but he didn't feel afraid. He trusted Tara's brother.

"Now, William, empty your mind of all other thoughts. Think only of my eyes ... only my eyes ... only my eyes ... " the fakir repeated quietly.

Goldenrod began to feel that he was floating. He was conscious only of the glowing green eyes, which seemed to be growing bigger. Then he heard the soft insistent voice say, "Now you will feel yourself becoming stronger and stronger ... stronger and stronger ... "

Each time the fakir said the word "stronger", Goldenrod felt tremendous power surge through his body. A few moments later he was convinced he had become immensely strong.

Then the fakir passed him a thick iron bar. It was about eighty centimetres long and four centimetres thick.

"Take this bar and bend it," the old man said softly.

Goldenrod gripped the bar at each end. With his new strength he was confident he would succeed. He paused for a moment, then squeezed his arms together and the iron bar bent into a U-shape just as if it was made of rubber.

The fakir folded his arms and watched his pupil with quiet satisfaction. As Goldenrod's newly found strength began to fade he felt very weak and tired, as the old man had foretold.

"You had better rest here for a while," the fakir said, pointing to a low couch. "It is important you remember how weak you feel now, so you will always carefully choose the time to call upon your extra strength. For an hour afterwards you will be very vulnerable."

"What does 'vulnerable' mean?"

"Open to attack by an enemy," the fakir replied. As he left the room, he closed the door behind him gently.

Goldenrod lay back on the couch and within seconds he fell into a deep sleep. After an hour he awoke feeling fully refreshed. He caught sight of the U-shaped iron bar lying on the floor and couldn't resist picking it up again He tried to straighten it, but without his special strength the task was a hopeless one.

The door opened slightly; the fakir peered through the small crack and, seeing Goldenrod was awake, came in to join him.

"William," he said, "I want you to come and see me as often as possible during the next few months, so that I can teach you to call upon your great strength all by yourself. When you come again I will explain everything to you."

Goldenrod thought how much he would enjoy showing his new strength to Subash and Fleabag.

"Can I tell anyone else about it?" he asked.

"Only your parents should know," the fakir replied, "and they will find out soon enough anyway. Probably during your first adventure."

Goldenrod went back upstairs for another talk with Tara. Soon afterwards his mother returned to take him home.

"I have invited William to come again soon," the fakir said to her. "I would like to see him as much as possible before you go to England."

"We won't be leaving India for many years," Mrs Rod said.

The fakir said nothing: he knew better. As they left, Goldenrod looked back and could see through the door that the old man was smiling to himself.

9
A Single Thought

About a week later Goldenrod went to see the fakir again. They sat cross-legged on the floor facing each other as the fakir explained to him how he could learn to acquire great strength whenever he was in danger.

"It is a question of concentrating your mind upon a single thought. In India we have a way of describing an undisciplined mind—it is one that flits from subject to subject like a monkey with St Vitus's dance that has just been stung by a wasp. Usually my pupils take many years to learn to think of a single thought or image, but I am going to hypnotise you again to make it much easier for you. Even so, you will still need to practise a great deal before you are able to do it on your own."

"How will thinking only one thought help me to become stronger when I need to?"

"As soon as someone can concentrate their mind all things are possible. By controlling their thoughts certain fakirs can walk on a bed of hot coals and feel no pain and others can be buried alive for many weeks. Becoming much stronger for a minute should be no problem once you can think of a single thought for long enough."

"How long is that?"

"Two-and-a-half minutes will be enough. It may not sound long, but when you first try, other thoughts will come into your mind within a few seconds."

Goldenrod found this very difficult to believe and was convinced he would last much longer.

"Let me try," he said.

He sat very still, closed his eyes and conjured up a picture of the fakir's face. Then he imagined the glowing green eyes and tried to think of nothing else. Within a few seconds he found himself wondering if Fleabag would come over on Saturday and what they would be having for tea.

He tried again, but this time he thought about Rajah's new collar, and then the back of his hand began to itch and he had to scratch it. He opened his eyes and the fakir smiled at him.

"It's much harder than I expected," Goldenrod said.

"Now I will hypnotise you. When you are in a trance I will suggest to your subconscious mind that you will find it easier to concentrate in future. I hope in this way we will reduce the learning period to under a year. Now, look into my eyes ... think only of my eyes ... only my eyes ... "

The fakir's soft voice kept repeating those words until Goldenrod was in a hypnotic trance. This time he could remember nothing that happened during it, but when he came out of the trance and tried to concentrate on a single thought again he found it far easier. The fakir told him that on one attempt he had lasted twenty seconds, which he said was very good for a beginner— even after hypnosis.

The fakir told Goldenrod to practise at home for about ten minutes before going to sleep at night and first thing in the morning. He also gave him some yoga exercises to do.

"As you learn to control your body better it will help you to control your mind," he said.

"My mother told me yoga took years to learn," Goldenrod replied.

"I am only giving you some very easy breathing exercises. They will help you to relax before you start to empty your mind and concentrate on a single thought."

"Is it true that some fakirs can breathe in one nostril and out of the other?"

"Yes, I can do that."

"Will you show me?"

"Not now," the fakir said smiling. "That is enough for one day. You go and see Tara—she has been looking forward to your visit."

During the weeks that followed, Goldenrod practised concentrating and worked hard at his yoga exercises. He visited the fakir and Tara several times and within six months he learned to concentrate upon the mental image of the fakir's glowing green eyes for nearly two minutes. Then one afternoon he managed the full two-and-a-half minutes. He knew he had lasted that long because it gave him a strange floating sensation, and he was suddenly conscious of being in complete control of his mind. The fakir was very pleased when he told him about it.

"You are ready for the next stage now," he said. "You will find that much easier. Once your mind is concentrated it is just a question of directing it, and having complete confidence that you will succeed. As soon as you feel that floating sensation you must start to tell yourself you are getting stronger and stronger. Keep say-

ing to yourself 'Stronger and stronger,' and you will soon begin to feel the strength surging into your body. Remember, though, it will only last for a minute, and afterwards you will feel very weak."

Goldenrod tried again to concentrate his mind on one image—the fakir's glowing green eyes. He lasted for two-and-a-half minutes and then he felt the strange floating sensation. This time he began to tell himself that he was becoming stronger and stronger and within a minute the surges of power started to shoot through his body. When he was at full strength the fakir passed him the U-shaped iron bar that he had bent six months earlier.

"Bend this back again," he said.

Goldenrod felt immensely powerful and straightened the iron bar without difficulty. As his strength began to fade he had to rest on the couch. When he awoke an hour later he felt completely refreshed.

When Goldenrod was ready to leave, the fakir went with him to the door. "Now my task is over," he said. "You are ready for your adventures, but it is vital you keep practising, and remember all I have taught you."

Then he paused for a few moments before making another prophecy: "Before the year is out you will be in great danger and may have to call upon your new strength more than once."

10

Farewell

Mrs Rod had lived in India long enough to know that fakirs were men of mystery who could foretell the future. She remembered that a year earlier the fakir had said he wanted to see as much of her son as possible before they went to England. Therefore it came as no surprise to her when Mr Rod received an unexpected offer of a position as the manager of a large farm in Sussex. He accepted right away; although he had enjoyed working in India, he liked the idea of returning to England and managing a farm there.

Goldenrod gave the news to his friends Subash and Fleabag.

"We'll miss you," Fleabag said.

"I wish I could come with you on the plane," Subash said. "I've never been on one."

"We came over from New York by jumbo jet," Fleabag said in a very superior tone. "After the first few hours it's pretty boring – I went to sleep some of the time."

"Will you be able to take Rajah?" Subash asked.

"Yes, we're taking him, but he'll have to go into quarantine for a few months. My father's going to explain it all to me."

"It'll be good fun on a farm with all those animals," Subash said.

"Yes, and next to us there's a training stables for race-horses," Goldenrod replied.

Then Fleabag had an inspiration. "You should have a goodbye party," he suggested.

Goldenrod mentioned Fleabag's idea to his mother, and before long the arrangements were in hand. Once again they had the snake-charmer and the man with the dancing bears. Goldenrod realised, as he watched them perform, that he might never see anything quite like it again. His parents had told him about the circuses in England, but they wouldn't be the same. Here in his own garden he felt that if he was unwise enough to want to, he could reach out and touch one of the snakes, or if one of the dancing bears took a liking to him, it might grab him in his arms. India was an exciting country to live in and he loved it in many ways.

The day before they left Goldenrod made a special journey to say goodbye to Tara and her brother.

"You're ready for your adventures now, chota sahib," she said, with tears in her eyes as she gave him a last hug.

"Thank you for everything," he replied, just managing not to cry. He turned to shake hands with her brother. "I'll write to you both often," he added.

The old man took the young boy's hand and looked deep into his eyes.

"Remember you must only use your powers to help others," he said. "That is why they have been given to you."

"I'll always remember," Goldenrod replied with quiet dignity. "Thank you for teaching me so much."

He found it difficult to say goodbye and was relieved when a few moments later his mother came to collect him.

The following day the Rod family and Rajah were driven by taxi to Delhi Airport, about sixteen kilometres outside New Delhi. Goldenrod had been there before, but never as a passenger. This time it was much more exciting; he was part of the hustle and bustle of hundreds of people going to so many different parts of the world.

They arrived an hour early, so they could deliver Rajah to the people in the cargo reception depot. Mr Rod supplied a special crate in which Rajah could travel in the plane's hold.

"He can't be with us, William," he explained. "They don't allow dogs on board with the passengers. You'll see him as soon as we arrive in London before he goes into quarantine."

"How long will he be in quarantine?"

"Six months – I know you'll miss him terribly, but we can't do anything about it. The authorities are very strict nowadays in trying to stop rabies and other infectious diseases from reaching England."

Rajah sensed that he was being talked about. A steward had arrived to lead him away, but Rajah resisted his efforts. He nuzzled his face against Goldenrod, who gave him a last hug, telling him not to worry and that he would see him soon. Then he said "Jow!" – the Hindi for "Go", one of the special words of command taught him by Pinukhan. Rajah gave him an imploring look, but seeing that his master was trying to look stern, he allowed the steward to lead him away.

A few days earlier Mr Rod had begun to explain the

quarantine procedure to his son. In particular he had reassured him that he would be able to visit Rajah while he was in the kennels. Even so, when the moment came to part from Rajah it was still a very unhappy one for the young boy.

"I don't see how keeping Rajah locked up for six months will help anybody," he muttered miserably.

"It helps because there are some terrible infectious diseases in India which animals in England don't get. If a dog travelling to England has been in contact with one of these illnesses, he may develop it after his arrival and infect other animals. But if he stays in quarantine for six months, a vet can keep an eye on him and treat any disease before it spreads. It's particularly important to stop rabies spreading because anyone who is bitten by a dog with rabies can easily die."

"But Rajah doesn't bite people."

"The trouble with rabies is that all dogs which contract it start biting people and other dogs without any reason. They don't know what they are doing."

"You mean if Rajah caught rabies he might bite me?" Goldenrod asked in amazement.

"Yes, even that could happen."

Mr Rod could see from his son's expression that, even though the six months would seem like an eternity to him, he was at last convinced quarantine was necessary for his dog.

After saying goodbye to Rajah, they checked in their baggage at the passenger desk and were handed their boarding passes. Then they waited in the main departure lounge until their flight was called.

"Will passengers for Trojan Airlines Flight TA713 please proceed to gate number 2 for security checks. The aircraft is now ready for boarding," a toneless voice announced over the loud speaker.

As they picked up their hand luggage and began to move towards gate 2, Goldenrod had a sudden feeling that he should turn back; he found it difficult to walk forward, almost as if the air in front of him had become thick and rubbery. He had been excited about flying to England, but now he felt uneasy. He was sure something would happen to them all if they set foot on the plane.

"Hurry up, William," his father said.

'No good saying anything,' Goldenrod thought. 'It must be because I haven't flown before.' He quickened his pace and caught up with his parents on their way to gate 2.

II

Take-off

Before they were allowed into the small passenger lounge their hand luggage and clothes were searched.

"Is this to stop hijackers?" Goldenrod asked excitedly.

"Yes, they always search everybody going on the plane to make sure they aren't carrying any weapons," Mr Rod replied.

"Why do people hijack planes—is it for money?"

"Not always. Sometimes the hijackers hold the passengers and crew hostage and threaten to shoot some of them if other terrorists aren't released from prison. It's very difficult then for the government of the country concerned to decide what to do. They don't want anyone to be shot and on the other hand they don't want to release the prisoners. If they raid the plane and attack the hijackers, there's always the risk of the passengers and crew being injured as well."

Goldenrod was silent as he thought about it.

"Don't worry, darling," Mrs Rod reassured him, "all the airport authorities are on the alert nowadays."

He smiled back at his mother to let her know that he wasn't frightened. He was a very logical boy and just liked to think problems right through to their solution.

After being searched they went to a small lounge where passengers for their flight were gathering. Goldenrod noticed two men talking intently together. The younger of them was wearing a light-grey suit; he was tall and thin, with dark hair smarmed down with too much hair lotion. But it was his glittering coal-black eyes that caught Goldenrod's attention. They were cruel

and cold, and one thing was certain: those eyes would never smile. The older man was quite different. Ill-at-ease in a crumpled blue suit, he looked like a retired boxer. He had a thick-set body, a craggy face with a big nose that had been badly broken and dull glazed pale-blue eyes. Although he was obviously much stronger than the younger man, it was clear who was the dominant personality – Craggy-Face, as Goldenrod christened him, was listening to every word the other man said.

Goldenrod rarely used his extraordinary hearing, especially to overhear other people's private conversations, but he felt he had to know what the two men were saying to each other. He sat down quietly and concentrated. Gradually he began to tune in to the sound of their voices.

"I'll go up first. You follow immediately I'm inside," the younger man was saying.

"What if there's a problem, Mr Manson?" Craggy-Face asked.

"You're being paid to deal with problems," was the harsh reply.

Some other passengers laughed loudly and Goldenrod missed the next few words. The two men moved away from each other, and sat separately while everyone waited for the ground hostess to tell them when their flight was ready to depart. Goldenrod thought about the fragment of conversation he had overheard; it seemed meaningless to him. He wondered if he should mention it to his father, but he knew Mr Rod wouldn't approve of his using his exceptional hearing to eavesdrop. Goldenrod decided to remain silent.

As the passengers boarded the plane he was disappointed to find that it was a Super VC–10. He'd hoped to fly in a jumbo jet. There were about 100 passengers in all and as the plane could carry over 135 there was plenty of room in both the first-class and economy cabins. Mr Rod's new employer was paying all the costs of their removal to England and they were lucky to be travelling first-class.

The cabin crew consisted of a chief steward, two male stewards and three hostesses, one of whom was Indian and wore a flowing red sari. The chief steward hovered between both cabins while a steward and one of the hostesses looked after the first-class passengers.

Mr and Mrs Rod were sitting together and Goldenrod's seat was just behind them, next to the gangway and right at the back. It took him by surprise when Craggy-Face came to sit next to him.

"Why don't you have the window seat while we take off?" he suggested. He had a friendly enough smile, but somehow Goldenrod didn't like him.

"That's good of you," Mr Rod said, turning round. "Why don't you, William? You'll be able to see the take-off much better."

"Thanks very much," Goldenrod replied as he moved over.

Of the twenty seats in the first-class compartment, five were empty. Across the gangway there was a very suntanned young man wearing a blazer and flannels. He was sitting quietly, fingers pressed together as if he was praying, and he seemed to be studying each of the passengers in turn, weighing them up carefully. Next to him a nun sat quietly reading a book. In front of her there was an elderly Indian businessman, a young European couple and an Italian lady with a girl of about sixteen. As the time for take-off approached, Goldenrod became more excited: his only disappointment was that Rajah couldn't be there to share his enjoyment.

The small signs saying "NO SMOKING: FASTEN SEAT BELTS" were already switched on. Then a woman's voice announced:

"Good afternoon, ladies and gentlemen. Welcome on board this Trojan Airlines Super VC–10. The aircraft is under the command of Captain Greaves. Our flight time to Doha will be three hours and forty minutes, and we shall be flying at an altitude of 35,000 feet. During the flight we shall be serving cocktails and lunch. Now will you please make sure that your seat belts are fastened, your tables are stowed and your seat backs are in the upright position ready for take-off. Thank you."

About ten minutes later, when they were just about to take off, the hostess gave them a final reminder. The plane began to trundle into position on the runway. There was a tremendous roar of jet engines, then it started to move forward, gradually gathering speed until suddenly, with a final lurch, they were airborne.

As the plane gained height, Goldenrod could see the airport, the roads around it and New Delhi itself gradually becoming smaller and smaller, before they finally faded into the distance. Soon they were flying above a sea of clouds, and Goldenrod noticed that the seat belt and no smoking signs had been switched off. Then over the loud speaker he heard the Captain say in a very relaxed voice:

"Good afternoon, ladies and gentlemen. This is Captain Greaves speaking. We are now flying at 35,000 feet. We have three hours to go before arriving in Doha, which means we'll be there at approximately three o'clock local time. There is a two-and-a-half hour time

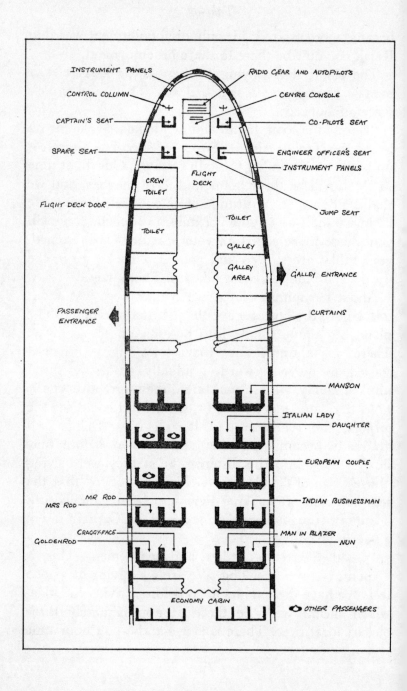

INSTRUMENT PANELS

RADIO GEAR AND AUTOPILOTS

CONTROL COLUMN

CENTRE CONSOLE

CAPTAIN'S SEAT

CO-PILOT'S SEAT

SPARE SEAT

ENGINEER OFFICER'S SEAT

INSTRUMENT PANELS

CREW TOILET

FLIGHT DECK

FLIGHT DECK DOOR

TOILET

JUMP SEAT

TOILET

GALLEY

GALLEY AREA

GALLEY ENTRANCE

PASSENGER ENTRANCE

CURTAINS

MANSON

ITALIAN LADY

DAUGHTER

EUROPEAN COUPLE

MR ROD

MRS ROD

INDIAN BUSINESSMAN

CRAGGY-FACE

MAN IN BLAZER

GOLDENROD

NUN

ECONOMY CABIN

OTHER PASSENGERS

change between Delhi and Doha, and if you would like to adjust your watches the time in Doha at the moment is five to twelve. The weather forecast for our route is fine, as is the forecast for Doha. I suggest that when you are in your seats you keep your seat belts fastened."

Goldenrod was so excited to be travelling in an airplane for the first time that he didn't notice the man next to him lean forward and take a small parcel from the pouch in the back of Mrs Rod's seat. Craggy-Face quickly put the package into his suit pocket, and looked around to make sure no one had seen him.

Shortly after they were airborne Goldenrod moved away from Craggy-Face to sit just across the gangway from his father, in the vacant seat next to the Indian businessman. The steward came round to check that everyone was comfortable. He was a short stocky man with ginger hair, who looked very smart in his white jacket and black bow-tie. He asked everyone to call him Peter, and explained to Goldenrod how to operate the reading light above his head, the little nozzle which blew cool air if he felt too hot and the knob to press when he wanted to push his seat back.

"You see that orange button above you," Peter said with a smile. "If you want me just push it, and I'll be along very quickly."

Goldenrod thanked Peter. He decided to read the book his aunt had sent him from England. It was *Charlie and the Great Glass Elevator*. He had enjoyed the first Charlie book about the chocolate factory and was looking forward to reading this one. He switched on his reading light and settled back in his seat, feeling very grown-up.

An hour later Peter and the hostess served lunch. Goldenrod had grapefruit cocktail and lamb with roast

F   77

potatoes and sprouts, followed by a delicious strawberry mousse. The Indian businessman said nothing to him as he ate his lunch, but Goldenrod chatted to his father across the gangway and Peter was very attentive.

"I've brought you an extra strawberry mousse," he said smiling. "You seemed to be enjoying it so much."

"Thanks, it's super," Goldenrod replied.

"And how about some more lemonade?" Peter asked.

"Yes, please."

Peter filled up Goldenrod's glass and moved on to speak to Craggy-Face.

"Is there anything more I can get you, sir?"

"No thanks," he replied gruffly.

He obviously didn't want to talk to anybody.

'He seems very tense,' Goldenrod thought. 'As if he's waiting for something.'

12

Hijacked

Lunch was soon cleared away. Goldenrod picked up his Charlie book again and soon forgot about Craggy-Face. He had been reading for about ten minutes when his father leant across to have a word with him.

"Are you enjoying it?" he asked.

"Yes, but not as much as the first one," he replied.

"No, I meant the flight," Mr Rod said. "Not the book."

"It's super. Fleabag said I'd be bored, but I'm not."

"There's a long way to go yet," Mr Rod replied, with a smile.

Goldenrod noticed the tall dark-haired man rise from his seat in the front of the cabin. At first he looked as if he might be going into the toilet, but he walked straight past to the door leading to the flight deck. He paused outside and looked through the small window. Then, without knocking, he went in and shut the door behind him.

Goldenrod narrowed his eyes and with his special vision he could see the Captain sitting to the left of the centre console, wearing a short-sleeved white shirt with gold epaulettes. On the right was the Co-pilot, with a

headset over his ears. Both he and the Engineer
Officer were busy with the instrument panels in front of
them.

Suddenly, to his horror, Goldenrod noticed that Mr
Manson had a small submachine-gun in his hand. He
pointed it at the back of the Captain's head. Goldenrod
concentrated hard and heard Manson speak.

"This is a hijacking," he said. "Do exactly as you are
told and you might live to tell the story. I want you to
change course ... "

Goldenrod's concentration was interrupted. Craggy-
Face was walking past him. 'What was it Manson had
said?' Goldenrod thought. '"I'll go up first, you follow
immediately I'm inside." No wonder Craggy-Face was
so tense.'

When he reached the front of the cabin Craggy-Face
turned and faced the passengers. He drew a revolver
from his suit pocket and pointed it down the gangway.

"Stay in your seats," he said menacingly.

Manson glanced through the window of the flight deck
door to check that Craggy-Face was in control. Then the
Captain's voice came over the loud speaker:

"Ladies and gentlemen: could I have your full attention please. This is an emergency. The plane has been
hijacked and we are being ordered to change course. I
am directed to tell you that any attempt by you to take
action of any kind will result in my being shot, and if that
happens the lives of all the passengers and crew will be
put in jeopardy. Please try to remain calm and stay in
your seats until I speak to you again."

The Captain's announcement was greeted by a
stunned silence, followed by a sudden babble of frightened
conversation. Mr Rod reassured his son before turning

to say a few words of comfort to his wife; the nun crossed herself and started praying; the young man in the blazer seemed unperturbed; the Indian businessman said something to himself in Hindi and the Italian lady started to laugh very loudly. Goldenrod heard someone say she had hysterics. It took her daughter ten minutes to calm her down, by which time her strange laughter had quietened the other passengers. In the silence that followed everyone was busy with their own thoughts.

Slowly Goldenrod began to recover from the shock of being hijacked.

'I must try and do something,' he thought. 'The fakir told me I should use my powers to help people. I wonder if he knew this was going to happen?

'The hijackers must have been working with someone who left the guns for them. Maybe it was one of the people who cleaned the plane.'

But then he had a more alarming thought.

'It could be one of the crew or a passenger. I didn't like the way the man in the blazer kept looking at everyone before we took off. He might be the one, but until I'm sure, there's nothing I can do about it.

'I must get nearer to Craggy-Face, use my strength on him and grab his gun. He won't expect me to try anything.'

Although Craggy-Face seemed rather dim, he looked very strong.

'I hope my strength lasts long enough or he'll murder me,' Goldenrod thought.

It took him a few minutes to master his fear and move into action.

"Please, sir, may I be excused?" he asked, putting up his hand just as he did when he was at school. Some of the other passengers laughed nervously and Mrs Rod looked across anxiously at her son.

"Okay," the hijacker said gruffly. "But be quick."

Goldenrod rose from his seat, walked slowly up to the front of the cabin and went into the toilet. He could see through the wall that the man was holding the gun in his left hand, which was nearer to him. If he could gather his strength and grab that hand he might be able to crush it before Craggy-Face had a chance to call Mr Manson.

Goldenrod noticed his heart was beating much louder than usual. 'I must keep calm,' he thought. He stood in front of the small mirror and did his yoga deep-breathing exercises. As he became more relaxed he began to clear his mind. 'I must think only of the fakir's glowing green eyes,' he kept saying to himself.

It was the first time he had tried to call up his great strength to deal with a dangerous person. He had a sudden thought: 'I hope the other hijacker doesn't join Craggy-Face.' It broke his concentration and he had to start again. 'I must think of only one thing,' he told himself. 'Only the fakir's eyes ... only his eyes ... only his eyes.'

Gradually Goldenrod began to feel the strange floating sensation as his mind emptied and all other thoughts were eliminated. After a few minutes he knew he was ready to summon his great strength – he concentrated on becoming stronger ... stronger ... stronger. Nothing happened for twenty seconds and then small surges of power began to flow through his body. They became greater and greater until he finally felt he was at full strength and ready to deal with the hijacker.

Goldenrod was aware that he only had one minute in which to render the man helpless. Quickly he opened

the door and as he walked quietly past Craggy-Face, he suddenly turned and clutched his hand. The hijacker was startled by the unexpected move; then his expression changed to one of horror as he realised that his hand was being crushed. He was a powerful man and couldn't believe a small boy could grip with such immense strength. As the pain increased he yelled out and then Goldenrod shoved him hard. He hit his head; the gun dropped from his nerveless fingers and Mr Rod sprang forward to grab it. Craggy-Face looked down dazedly at his bruised hand as Mr Rod pushed him into a nearby seat. The hijacker slumped back heavily, his head lolling to one side, as he lost consciousness.

It was all so fast that none of the other passengers realised what had happened. Some of them had seen Goldenrod clutch the hijacker's hand, but it was un-believable that a small boy could have really hurt him. They thought that he must just have startled the hijacker and then Mr Rod had been very quick to grab his gun.

"William," his father said quietly, "I don't know how you did that, but I'm very proud of you."

Goldenrod smiled wearily; already he was beginning to feel weak and the second, far more dangerous hijacker still had to be dealt with.

13
The Accomplice

Goldenrod narrowed his eyes and looked through the door which led to the flight deck. Manson was still standing behind the Captain. As if he sensed someone was looking at him, the hijacker turned around and strode to the small window. Mr Rod had realised that it would be only a matter of minutes before Manson found out what had happened to Craggy-Face. He was ready for him. Quickly he held a magazine over the outside of the window to block Manson's view. Goldenrod could see through it that the hijacker was furious and had turned back to talk to the Captain.

Waves of tiredness began to engulf Goldenrod.

"I must rest now," he said to his father, as he stumbled to his seat. Within seconds he was fast asleep.

The Captain's tense voice came over the public address system:

"Ladies and gentlemen: I must have your full attention. I am directed to advise you that unless you do exactly as instructed all of your lives will be in great danger. The hijacker requires his associate to be released immediately, the gun in your possession to be handed back and the obstruction to be removed from the window. He has asked me to explain to you that if you try to use the gun, there is a severe risk of breaking a window and causing total decompression of this aircraft. In that event passengers could be sucked out of the plane and many lives lost. The hijacker has also told me that if his instructions aren't obeyed to the letter within the next ten minutes, he will shoot me and my Co-pilot. This will inevitably result in all passengers losing their lives. I urge you to carry out his instructions immediately.''

The Captain knew that it was Trojan Airlines' policy in the case of hijacking to do everything possible to preserve the lives of the passengers. They urged the crew not to try and be heroes, and to leave it to the authorities to decide how to deal with hijackers. The Captain had been told that it was very important not to argue unnecessarily, to speak clearly and to move very slowly and deliberately, as hijackers were often desperate men fully prepared to risk their own lives. Of course, he had taken the standard precaution of quietly changing the setting on the transponder, so that an emergency radar pulse was already being transmitted on a special frequency. The course of the plane was no doubt being plotted by the authorities below, but no one would interfere until they knew the hijackers' demands.

Mr Rod only had ten minutes. He glanced at his son, who was in a blissful sleep.

'William won't be able to help this time,' Mr Rod thought. 'I must try and work out a plan. First I'll stick something over this window. That will make me more mobile. Then I'll find out if any of the passengers can handle a gun.'

Mr Rod secured a page of the magazine over the small window.

"I'm hopeless with guns—are you a good shot?" he asked the young man in the blazer, who had come up to the front of the cabin.

"No, I'm afraid not," he replied.

"I am," Peter, the steward, said confidently. "Perhaps I can help."

Mr Rod passed him the revolver.

"I don't know what we're going to do," he said. "But one thing is certain—if you use that gun you'll have to be dead accurate."

The expression on Peter's face changed.

"I'll be accurate all right," he said, pointing the gun at Mr Rod. "Go back to your seats and sit down immediately."

Mr Rod was staggered. Peter was the hijackers' accomplice. He must have brought the guns on the plane for them.

Mr Rod and the young man returned to their seats, and Peter tore down the piece of paper covering the flight deck window. Manson opened the door and joined him.

"What's happened to Fred?" he asked.

Peter went up to have a closer look at Craggy-Face, who was slumped in the front seat. He shook him gently, but there was no response.

"Somehow that boy and his father got hold of his gun. He bashed his head. He's dead to the world now."

"You'd better take this gun. I'll use the revolver," Manson said. "Leave this communicating door open and keep the stewards and hostesses in their seats. It's easier to control everyone that way. You can see right down the plane from here."

Manson returned to the flight deck and shortly after-

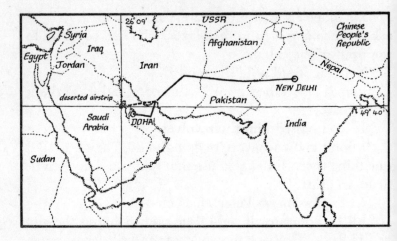

wards the Captain's voice came over the loud speaker.

"Ladies and gentlemen: in approximately one hour's time we will be landing at an airstrip in Saudi Arabia. I am directed to advise you that anyone attempting to interfere again will be shot. I urge you to keep calm, remain in your seats and take no further action until I speak to you again. When we have landed we will radio the authorities in London and, if they agree to the hijackers' demands, all of us will be released immediately. I hope to be allowed to speak to you again shortly, but in the meantime please fasten your seat belts and put out your cigarettes. Thank you."

There was a nervous buzz of conversation and then the passengers fell silent, except for occasional whispers. Goldenrod woke from his deep sleep to find the hijackers firmly back in control. In a low voice Mr Rod briefly explained to him what had happened.

"I'm sorry it was Peter," Goldenrod said. "I liked him."

"So did I," Mr Rod whispered. "But at least we know

who it is now. Unfortunately we're unlikely to get a second chance to turn the tables."

Peter's suspicions were aroused.

"Stop talking, you two," he said.

Mr Rod smiled reassuringly at his son, and settled back in his seat. Only one factor remained in their favour – the hijackers had no way of knowing that one of the passengers had special powers.

14
Rough Landing

Goldenrod felt a strange sensation in his ears, which he knew was due to the change of pressure as the plane descended rapidly. It circled twice before attempting to land on the old airstrip. At the last moment it veered away. Goldenrod could see the Captain and Manson were arguing, so he used his special hearing to tune in on their conversation.

"I can't land there—it's far too dangerous," the Captain said. "There are craters and large cracks on that runway—it hasn't been used for years and I doubt if it was ever used for a plane of this size."

"There are degrees of danger," Manson replied, smiling evilly. "You should consider the alternative."

"What do you mean?" the Captain asked.

"Simply this—if you don't land on that runway I'm going to pull this trigger and blow your head off. You have exactly one minute to decide whether or not you think I'm bluffing," Manson said, looking at his watch and taking a careful note of the position of the second hand.

The Captain was a courageous man and might have taken the risk, if he had only himself to worry about. He knew, however, that his main responsibility was for the lives of the passengers and crew.

"You win," he said. "But I must warn the passengers and tell them to prepare for a very rough landing."

"Okay," Manson replied. "Go ahead."

The Captain spoke slowly and deliberately into the public address system:

"Ladies and gentlemen: this is an emergency announcement. I regret to advise you that the condition of the runway is poor and it is essential that you prepare yourselves for a very rough landing. Please take off ties, loosen collars and remove dentures, glasses, and high-heeled shoes. Check your seat belts are fastened tightly, tables are stowed and your chair-back is in the upright position. Then place your feet squarely on the floor, hold your pillow on your knees and put one arm under it. Bend forward and rest your head on the pillow and place your other hand firmly on the top of your head

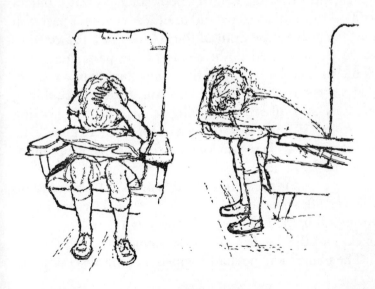

ready for impact. I will do my best to ensure a safe landing."

There was a nervous buzz of response from the passengers as they began to follow the Captain's instructions. The Indian businessman took off his tie and glasses, and carefully removed his false teeth. Then he turned to look at Goldenrod with what was probably meant to be a reassuring smile. In spite of the gravity of the situation Goldenrod nearly burst out laughing. 'He looks just like Popeye,' he thought.

Within a few minutes everyone was crouched down in their seats, strangely silent as they began once more to circle the runway. Every second seemed like a minute. The plane continued to lose height and then Goldenrod felt a sudden jarring shock as the Super VC–10 touched the ground. It landed hard and bounced badly several times as it gradually juddered to a halt. Goldenrod heard a crash which sounded like some bottles breaking in the galley, and saw his Charlie book slide forward out of sight. Then a black shoe and another book shot past him on their way to the front of the cabin. For a few seconds there was an awed hush. Many of the passengers were silent in thankful prayer that they had landed safely and were still alive. Then there was a sudden babble of noise as they all started talking to each other, checking up to see if anyone had been injured. Fortunately no bones were broken and only a few people had minor cuts and bruises.

Goldenrod glanced out of the window. There were no signs of life and the ground was bare and brown in the strong sunlight. The only building was a derelict concrete one about the size of a very small bungalow.

The plane's engines had stopped and the air-conditioning system was no longer working. As Goldenrod began to feel warmer, he suddenly remembered poor Rajah in the hold. Even if Rajah had escaped injury, he wouldn't survive in that heat without air-conditioning. He had to do something quickly.

Just at that moment the Italian lady started talking in a loud voice to her daughter. Then her strange laughter began again. The other passengers became very quiet as the eerie sound echoed through the plane.

"What's she on about?" Manson asked, coming from the flight deck.

"The girl speaks English — I'll try and find out," Peter replied. After a few minutes, with the daughter's help, he discovered that the Italian lady had a small poodle in the hold. Nothing would console her — she was sure that her poodle would die unless they could release him.

Goldenrod acted quickly. He put up his hand to attract Peter's attention.

"Please, Peter," he called out, "my dog's in the hold too. He might die in this heat. Is there any way we can get him out?"

Manson realised he had to do something to keep the passengers calm and under his control. The lady's cries were upsetting everyone — they had even put his own nerves on edge.

"How do you get into the hold?" he asked Peter.

"There's a trap door into the electrics bay, and that leads into number one hold," Peter said, pointing towards the entrance.

"Okay," Manson said to him. "Get one of the stewards to go down and let the dogs out."

The trap door was opened and a steward soon returned with Rajah and a black poodle. The Italian lady immediately became calmer, embraced her small dog and began to speak comfortingly to it in Italian. Rajah bounded forward to greet Goldenrod, delighted to be reunited with his master, who quickly checked that he was in good fettle.

"Now listen," Manson said to Peter. "I'll radio London and issue our ultimatum. You keep an eye on the passengers. I won't close the door in case there's more trouble."

Manson covered the flight deck crew with his revolver, leaving Peter with the powerful submachine-gun to control everyone else. Mr Rod wondered if he should take any action against the hijacker—clearly, if a number of the passengers rushed Peter, they could easily overwhelm him. Then he began to count the difficulties:

1 The gangway was quite narrow and Peter could easily shoot anybody trying to approach him.
2 They had been told that everyone would be released if the authorities agreed to the hijackers' demands. Most of the passengers would think they were unlikely to be harmed if they did nothing.
3 Very few people are ever prepared to risk their own lives.

Mr Rod knew there would have been a rush to the front of the gangway if Peter had been offering champagne and caviar to the first passengers to reach him. But being shot is different. Mr Rod realised that there was nothing he could do.

15
A Special Word

As Manson began to talk to the Captain, Goldenrod used his extraordinary hearing to listen in on them:

"I want you to radio London and make sure your company delivers this message to the authorities," the hijacker said, passing the Captain a sheet of paper covered in typing.

"It's far too long," Captain Greaves replied. "Our batteries will only last half an hour. I'll have to work on it and cut down the number of words."

"All right, but hurry."

Captain Greaves amended Manson's message and passed it back to him for approval.

"That's okay," Manson replied. "Now before you transmit, press the loud-speaker button, so that I can hear London as well."

The Captain passed Manson's message to the Co-pilot, who bent over the radio equipment on the centre console and began to transmit.

"Trojan London. This is Trojan 657 on 8846. Do you read?"

There was a moment's silence followed by the crackling sound of static electricity. Then a faint voice replied:

95

"Trojan 657. This is Trojan London. Go ahead."

"Trojan London. Trojan 657. We have been hijacked. Hijacker demands that authorities release George Staunton from ... "

The faint voice interrupted.

"Trojan 657. Trojan London. Say again name after 'release'."

"Trojan London. Trojan 657. GEORGE STAUNTON: Golf, Echo, Oscar, Romeo, Golf, Echo. GEORGE. Sierra, Tango, Alpha, Uniform, November, Tango, Oscar, November. STAUNTON from Pentonville prison. Deliver Staunton by small aircraft with half a million pounds in krugerrands. Our position is deserted airstrip, Saudi Arabia; 26°09′ North, 49°40′ East. Runway in bad condition. This aircraft slightly damaged. Will switch radios on in one hour at 14.00G, when hijacker expects confirmation his demands will be met. If not, hijacker will shoot three passengers every hour. Also any other attempt to approach aircraft will result in passengers being shot immediately. Over."

"Trojan 657. Trojan London. Stand by."

"He's checking over the message and he'll probably ring his boss to find out what to do," Captain Greaves said slowly to reassure the hijacker.

A few minutes later they heard the faint voice from London again.

"Trojan 657. Trojan London. Roger. Wilco."

"That means the message has been understood and will be acted upon," Captain Greaves informed the hijacker.

Goldenrod was chilled with fear as he thought about Manson's words. He wondered if the authorities in London would agree to the hijackers' demands. Five hundred thousand pounds was a great deal of money and they wouldn't want to release a prisoner: Staunton was probably a very dangerous man. Manson hadn't given them much time to make up their minds—already five minutes of the hour had gone. If London didn't agree, whom would Manson shoot first? His father had already upset the hijackers—he could easily be one of the first three passengers to be shot.

Goldenrod shuddered at the thought. He knew that he mustn't panic. He had to think calmly and try to work out a plan. If he could catch one of the hijackers off guard his special strength would be enough to deal with him. But afterwards he would feel weak and tired, and the other hijacker would be able to regain control.

Peter the steward looked as if he knew how to handle the submachine-gun. The situation seemed hopeless; but Goldenrod still searched for an answer. His greatest friend was lying asleep by his side, blissfully unaware that his master was in any danger. The thought of his dog gave Goldenrod an inspiration—Rajah was the key to the problem. A plan began to take shape in his mind: step one, waken Rajah without arousing suspicion; step two, persuade Rajah that Peter was playing the gun game with him just like Pinukhan used to back home in India; step three, say the word of command; step four, try to grab the gun before Manson intervened. It was a good plan because, even if he couldn't get Peter's gun, he'd still have his special strength in reserve.

Another ten minutes had passed. Manson was still occupied on the flight deck talking to the Captain about water supplies. It was now or never. Goldenrod casually dropped his arm over the edge of his seat and began to stroke Rajah's head. There was no response—Rajah liked being stroked and hoped Goldenrod would continue as long as possible. The stroke became a nudge, and then the nudge became a discreet thump. Rajah decided he had better wake up. As he opened his eyes he caught sight of Peter's feet ahead of him in the gangway. His master was leaning down and whispering to him. "Pinukhan, Pinukhan, Pinukhan." He looked up at Peter and was disappointed to see that he wasn't at all like Pinukhan. His master was holding his head firmly so he couldn't look round at the other passengers. Anyway, his sense of smell always told him if anyone he knew was nearby. Rajah wondered why his master kept saying the name Pinukhan; he was wrong this time, Pinukhan wasn't there.

Rajah couldn't understand why his head was being gripped so tightly—almost as if he was being pointed at something. Then he noticed the man in front of him had

a submachine-gun in his hands. The threatening way he was holding it coupled with the sound of Pinukhan's name made him react automatically: within a second he was poised and quivering, waiting for the special word of command. Sensing that he was ready, Goldenrod released his grip on Rajah, who crouched beside him staring up at Peter.

"Your dog's giving me a funny look," Peter said. "Is he all right?"

"He's fine—he's just waiting for me to say a special word," Goldenrod said innocently.

"What word's that?" Peter asked.

"*Halma!*"

Rajah sprang forward like a ground-to-air missile. Over thirty kilos of bone and muscle connected with the startled Peter. Rajah's teeth closed around his wrist and, as he tried to fight him off, he dropped the gun. Mr Rod

sprang from his seat and picked it up. Manson was taken by surprise and reacted slowly. He was too late to intervene; all he could do was quickly slam the communicating door, secure it from the inside, and close the shutter across the small window.

Goldenrod said "Neachu!" and Rajah released Peter and came back to his master's side, wagging his tail and obviously very pleased with himself.

"Well done, Rajah," Mr Rod said as he pushed Peter firmly into a nearby seat where he could keep an eye on him. He made him fasten his seat belt tightly, gagged him with his own handkerchief and secured his hands with a long piece of string they found in the galley.

Mr Rod had a quick word with the young man in the blazer who seemed eager to help.

"I'll stay here in case Manson tries to take us by surprise," he said. "You go down the plane, tell all the passengers exactly what's happened and ask them to stay calm."

"Good news travels fast," the young man replied. "I think they already know, but I'll make sure."

Goldenrod stayed with his father and narrowed his eyes to look through the door. He could see that the hijacker still had the gun in his hand covering the flight deck crew, who were being forced to stay in their seats and look straight ahead. Goldenrod used his special hearing to find out what he was saying to them.

"London won't realise what's happened. They'll still send the plane and I'll use you three as hostages," Manson said. "If the passengers make a rescue attempt all of you will be shot and before I get killed I'll make sure I take some of them with me. Tell them now—and remember, no funny business."

A Special Word

The Captain spoke into the public address system: "Ladies and gentlemen: this is Captain Greaves. The hijacker has instructed me to tell you that he will shoot me, my Co-pilot and the Engineer Officer if any attempt is made to rescue us. He has also threatened to shoot some of you. I urge you to take whatever action you consider necessary ... "

The last few words were blurted out quickly before Manson realised that he was dealing with a very brave man. Quickly he knocked out the Captain with his revolver. Then Manson's harsh voice came over the loud speaker:

"Make your own decision, but remember the lives of three men and some of yours will depend on it being right. If you take no action until a plane arrives to take me to another destination no one will be harmed. It's up to you."

Not one passenger thought that Manson was bluffing. Everything about him was evil. He wouldn't hesitate to kill.

16

Strange Weapon

Goldenrod could see that Manson was leaning back against the door at the rear of the flight deck.

"Dad," he said, "if we could find a thick iron bar or something like that, I could drive it through this window and hit the back of Manson's head. It might knock him out before he could hurt the pilots."

Mr Rod was very impressed by his son's quiet confidence; he realised he had something very special about him. There were so many questions he wanted to ask, but they would have to wait. Right now they still had to deal with Manson. It had occurred to Mr Rod that he might be able to shoot Manson through the door, but that would risk injuring the crew. He was very anxious to avoid extreme violence if at all possible. The idea of shooting another man appalled him. He might be able to bring himself to do it as a last resort, but only to save lives.

"Right, William," he replied. "You're thinking on the right lines, but the difficulty will be to find something that won't break on impact. The shutter behind the glass looks as if it's made of metal. We'd better talk to the others and see if anyone can find a suitable weapon. I'll pretend I'm going to do it."

When the young man returned, Mr Rod explained the plan to him and some of the other passengers.

"It looks impossible to me," one of them said. "Are you sure you're strong enough?"

"My son will help me," Mr Rod replied. The passengers thought Mr Rod was just being kind mentioning him. They would have been very surprised to learn that it was Goldenrod who would be trying to save them all.

"What we need now is a weapon," Mr Rod said to the young man in the blazer. "I'd better stay here and keep an eye on the door in case Manson tries anything. You see if you can find something suitable."

"Shall I start in the hold?" the young man asked.

"I'd try the galley first. Then go down the plane and check with the passengers one by one—you might find something in their hand luggage."

Goldenrod helped look in the galley, but the search was unsuccessful. Then the young man began to move down the gangway checking with the passengers individually. Craggy-Face was still unconscious in the front seat and next to him sat Peter, bound and gagged.

The Italian lady and the European couple had nothing to offer, but the Indian businessman had an idea.

"I'm a keen amateur photographer," he said. "I've brought my tripod on the plane because I didn't want it damaged in the hold. It's made of steel so it should be strong enough."

The young man lifted the tripod down from the rack. "Many thanks. I think this might do," he said as he carried it back for Mr Rod to inspect.

"Yes," Mr Rod said. "That's just the kind of thing I'm looking for. I'll strip it down. With the legs bunched together it should do the trick."

Mr Rod quickly prepared the tripod for action.

"Could you persuade everyone to return to their seats?" he asked the young man. "After that it'll be better if you stay at the front of the gangway, and keep an eye on these two," he added, pointing at Craggy-Face and Peter.

Goldenrod remained with his father.

"I think we should pull the curtains," he said to him. "The fakir told me not to let other people know about my powers."

Mr Rod agreed and pulled the grey curtains together. He smiled at his son.

"What happens now?" he asked.

"I need a few minutes to gather my strength."

With his special vision he looked through into the flight deck. The hijacker was still leaning back against the wall, gun in hand. Goldenrod made sure that the tripod was nearby before he began to relax and empty his mind.

Again he thought of the glowing green eyes of the fakir ... only the eyes ... only the eyes. After about fifty seconds he found himself worrying about what he would do if Manson moved during the next few minutes. 'This is no good,' he thought, 'I must concentrate.' He tried again and this time it was a little better and then just near the end he thought about the tripod and began to wonder if it would break on impact.

Then he had the most worrying thought of all: he had never before used his power twice in a single day. Would he be able to concentrate sufficiently the second time? The fakir had said that "before the year is out" he might have to use his strength "more than once", but he hadn't said anything about its being in a single day.

Goldenrod knew that his only hope was positive thinking ; remembering his yoga exercises he began to breathe slowly and deeply and as he relaxed he concentrated on the glowing green eyes. After a few minutes of intense mental effort he was elated to feel the floating sensation. He started to summon his strength, and the response was immediate. The familiar surges of power began to flow through his body. When his strength was at its height, he turned to his father.

"I only have a minute," he said.

"I've found this metal box in the galley," Mr Rod replied. "I've put it down here for you to stand on."

"That's a good idea," Goldenrod said. "Will you hold me steady?"

His father gripped his son's hips firmly with both hands. Goldenrod used his special sight to check Manson's exact position.

"He's moved," he said to his father. "He's at least half a metre away from the door now."

"Can you still do it?"

"I'm not sure. I've only a few seconds left. I'll try it at full strength."

Goldenrod drew back his arms and with a sudden surge of tremendous power he drove the strange weapon straight at the small metal window.

At that precise moment the hijacker was thinking he might manage to escape, as he doubted if the passengers would risk their own lives and those of the crew. A fraction of a second later he heard an explosive crash, as the glass window shattered, the metal shutter was torn away and the tripod burst through into the flight deck. As it connected with the top of his spine, he felt a piercing pain – and that was the last thing he knew until three

days later, when he regained consciousness in a prison hospital.

Goldenrod stepped down from the box and when the grey curtains were drawn back it appeared to the other passengers that Mr Rod was the hero of the day. If they had known that it was the tired young boy with golden hair who had saved them all, he would have become the subject of world-wide curiosity. It was far better to keep quiet about it.

The passengers were crowding around Mr Rod, wanting to hear the full story. The Captain, who had recovered from his beating, quickly contacted London to give them the good news. Then he came through from the flight deck.

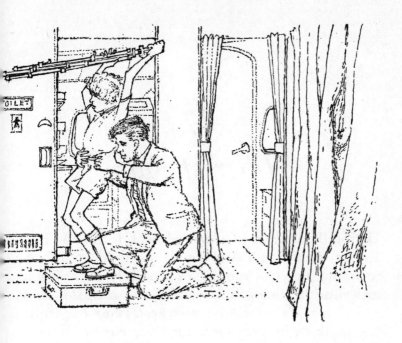

"How did you manage to drive that tripod through the door?" he asked.

"My son helped me," Mr Rod replied smiling. The passengers laughed: they all thought he was joking and being modest. The real hero of Flight TA713 was already back in his seat fast asleep. Rajah was perched on the seat beside him, watching over his master–no one was going to put him back in the hold again.

17

Hillcrest Farm

During the time that Goldenrod slept, trucks and Land
Rovers of the Saudi Arabian army moved up to begin
repairing the old runway. Then a large helicopter
arrived with Saudi Arabian police, who carried Manson
and Craggy-Face away on stretchers. Peter, handcuffed
and looking very sorry for himself, was escorted from the
plane to the helicopter. As it receded into the distance
that was the last any of the passengers saw of the hijackers, who, several months later, stood trial and were
all given long prison sentences.

A small plane arrived with a team of maintenance
men, who checked over the VC–10. Captain Greaves
then taxied his plane off the runway. A few minutes later
he made his final announcement to the passengers:

"Ladies and gentlemen: could I have your attention
please. On behalf of Trojan Airways I should like to
apologise to you for all you have been through during the
last few hours. In spite of security precautions I'm afraid
these things still happen occasionally. At least we can all
be thankful that there's been no loss of life and none of
you has been seriously injured.

"Another VC–10 will be landing here. You'll be

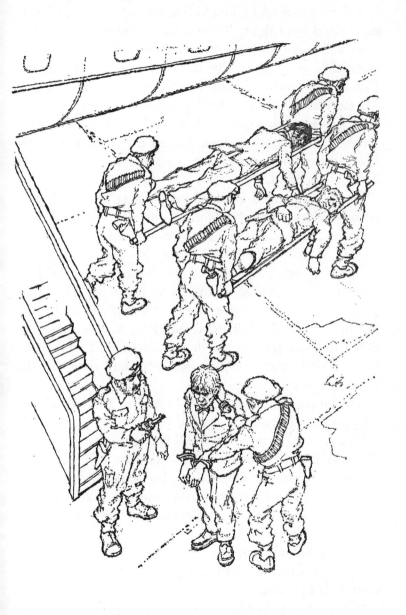

transferred to it and taken to Bahrain where you will stay in a hotel overnight. Tomorrow morning Trojan Airways will arrange for you to carry on to your destinations as quickly as possible. Thank you for your co-operation. I'm sure you will all wish to join me in congratulating Mr Rod for his part in dealing with the hijackers. Without his intervention it might have ended very differently."

The Indian businessman leaned across to thank Mr Rod and several other passengers came up and shook him by the hand.

When Goldenrod awoke from his sleep it had already become dark. The transfer to the other plane went smoothly, and, because of the very exceptional circumstances, Rajah was allowed to stay in the cabin with his master. When they arrived in Bahrain a crowd of reporters was waiting to interview Mr Rod. They had already heard something about his exploits and were anxious to get the full story. Mr Rod was very modest about his own part in the drama and didn't let anyone know that it was really his son who had defeated the hijackers.

The following morning, over breakfast, Goldenrod told his parents all about his special powers.

"You must promise me you'll be careful when you use them, William," Mrs Rod said anxiously. To his mother, whatever powers he might have, he would always be the son she loved and felt protective towards.

Mr Rod smiled at his wife's concern. "He knows what he's doing," he said proudly.

"The fakir told me you'd learn all about my powers, but he said I mustn't let other people know," Goldenrod warned his parents.

"Don't worry, William," his father replied. "We won't

tell anyone. Let's hope it will be a long time before you have to use them again. If you do, and you want any help from me, you only have to say the word."

The way Goldenrod and his father had worked together against the hijackers had brought them very close to each other. But now their adventure was behind them they were dropping back into a normal father and son relationship.

The journey to London was uneventful. After they had been through customs Goldenrod went to say an unhappy farewell to his dog. There was no way that he could explain to him why they had to be parted again. Neither of their lives would be complete until they were reunited.

"I'll come and see you as often as I can," Goldenrod called to Rajah, who looked back at him dejectedly as he was led off to quarantine.

Goldenrod and his parents went by car from Heathrow Airport to Hillcrest Farm near Midhurst in Sussex. As he entered the old house on top of the hill overlooking the 3,000-acre farm, Goldenrod knew that he was going to be happy there. He loved animals, especially dogs and horses. His father had told him there was a training stables for race-horses nearby; he hoped the people would be friendly and invite him to have a look around one day. Goldenrod had no way of knowing then that he would soon be a regular visitor to the Thompson stables and become very fond of a famous race-horse. Only his efforts and those of Rajah would interfere with the plans of a gang of criminals known as The Syndicate ... But that's another story.

International Aviation Phonetic Alphabet

English is the main language used in civil aviation. If, for example, a Dutch non-military plane was flying over Italy, the pilot would speak in English and expect to be answered in it.

The only exception to this general practice is when nationals are flying over their own country. For instance, a Danish pilot flying over Denmark would speak in Danish.

It was not always easy to understand the normal pronunciation of A,B,C, so a phonetic alphabet was invented. At first A was Ack and B was Beer. Then A became Able and B was changed to Baker.

The phonetic alphabet in use at present is as follows:

A	lpha	I	ndia
B	ravo	J	uliet
C	harlie	K	ilo
D	elta	L	ima
E	cho	M	ike
F	oxtrot	N	ovember
G	olf	O	scar
H	otel	P	apa

Q	uebec	V	ictor
R	omeo	W	hisky
S	ierra	X	ray
T	ango	Y	ankee
U	niform	Z	ulu

The words are chosen for the way they sound and in most cases the endings are very different and distinctive.

The phonetic alphabet has many uses. A pilot giving his aircraft registration would not say G–ASGW; he would spell it out as Golf, Alpha, Sierra, Golf, Whisky. Also, if the receiver does not understand part of a message, the person transmitting it will repeat the difficult words phonetically. In this way aircraft all over the world are able to communicate with ground control and with each other.

The Meaning of the Indian Words and the More Difficult English and Other Words Used in the Story

Note The meaning given only refers to the way in which a word is used in the story. Many words have several different meanings and for a fuller understanding you will need a dictionary.

accomplice:	partner in crime; fellow criminal
antibiotics:	powerful medicines able to destroy almost all germs except viruses
ayah:	Indian nanny
casual:	unconcerned, not worried (p. 19); as if by chance (p. 99)
caviar:	a luxury food – the pickled roe, or eggs, of the sturgeon, a large fish
chalna:	walk
chota sahib:	little master
concentrate:	think hard about one particular thing

decompression:	reduction of air pressure
dignity:	self-respect and pride
discreet:	cautious
distinction:	difference from others, mark of honour
dominant:	having power, commanding
eerie:	strange, weird
eliminate:	get rid of
engulf:	swallow up, cover completely
eternity:	time that has no end
fakir:	holy man, possessed of miraculous powers such as walking on fire
fettle:	condition
frail:	weak, easily broken
handicap:	disadvantage, something that makes life difficult for a person
hazard:	obstacle, something in the way
hysterics:	fit of uncontrollable laughter or weeping
image:	picture in the mind
initiative:	enterprise, imagination
inspiration:	a sudden bright idea
instalment:	one of several parts of something that goes on over a period of time
intently:	giving close attention
intervene:	come between people in a dispute

Vocabulary

jeopardy:	danger
juldi:	quickly
knack:	clever way of doing something
krugerrand:	South African gold coin
listless:	not wanting exercise, uninterested
logical:	clear-thinking, able to reason
memsahib:	madam, lady
monsoon:	seasonal wind, in summer accompanied by rain
operable:	can be operated upon
ophthalmic:	of the eye
pension:	a regular payment made by a former employer to a person who is disabled, old, or a widow of a former employee
permeate:	spread through
pronunciation:	the sound of the spoken word
retinas:	coatings at the back of the eyeball sensitive to light
sari:	a long silk or cloth wrapping worn by Indian women
sensation:	feeling
siesta:	afternoon rest in hot countries
simmer:	keep on the point of boiling
spur of the moment:	suddenly

Vocabulary

subconscious: part of the mind which is not fully aware but which can affect our actions

surges: waves

tension: nervous strain, worry

trance: condition of being unaware of what is going on around you

transponder: device for receiving a radio signal and automatically transmitting a different signal

ultimatum: list of demands sent by one party to another with notice that they must be met within a fixed time

undisciplined: untrained, uncontrolled

vague: not clear or distinct

virus: minute germ which is the cause of many infections such as the common cold, influenza and polio

vivid: bright

yoga: system of exercises teaching control of the mind and body